A stranger

"SOL2? Are those someone's initials?"

"No, actually, SOL2 stands for Sons of Liberty Two. The second coming of the original Sons of Liberty, in a way. You probably learned about the first Sons in school—Sam Adams, Paul Revere, those guys?"

"Sure," I said. "There were lots of different groups of them, weren't there? Sort of like secret societies?"

Cam nodded. "Same deal here," he said. "The movement's in its infancy, just taking shape. I think it's got some real potential. There may be a place for me in all this."

No, I thought, although it certainly was my older brother that we'd found, this seemed to be a…how shall I put it?…different *version* of the guy. A Cam who didn't seem quite right to me.

BROTHERS

Julian F. Thompson

A KNOPF PAPERBACK
ALFRED A. KNOPF • NEW YORK

For Polly and for Reggie, my refreshers,
my sustainers, and my loves

A KNOPF PAPERBACK PUBLISHED BY ALFRED A. KNOPF

www.randomhouse.com/kids

Library of Congress Cataloging-in-Publication Data
Thompson, Julian F.
Brothers / Julian F. Thompson.
p.   cm.
Summary: When his idolized older brother leaves college for a mental health
facility and then disappears, seventeen-year-old Chris follows him to the
compound of an anti-government militia group and tries to rescue him.
[1. Militia movements—Fiction. 2. Brothers—Fiction. 3. Mentally ill—Fiction.]
I. Title.
PZ7.T371596Br   1998
[Fic]—dc21   98-11001

ISBN 0-679-89082-3 (trade)
ISBN 0-679-99082-8 (lib. bdg.)
ISBN 0-375-80353-X (pbk.)

First Knopf Paperback edition: May 2000
Printed in the United States of America
10 9 8 7 6 5 4 3 2 1

chapter 1

Once upon a time, we called each other "frah-tair."

That dated back to when he found himself in first-year Latin, and he learned the word for brother: *frater*. He told me I could call him that instead of Cam. He pronounced it slowly for me: "frah-tair."

"See how special that'll be?" he'd said. Even then he could project excitement like no other person I've ever met. He does it with his voice and a look that he gets in his eyes. He makes you want to tell him yes, and yes, and YES! I've tried to borrow it, that . . . attribute of his, and run it at the girls I'd like to do things with, but I can't bring it off. They know it isn't me; I think they think I've seen too many movies.

"You're the only person in the world who has the right to call me that," he'd told me. "And even if you live to be C-X-X-V, you'll never have a frater just like me, one with the exact same bloodline."

I knew CXXV was a hundred and twenty-five because he'd already taught me Roman numerals. I was VIII that year, and he was XII. Our father had died two years before, and there was only Mom and Cam and me. So by the time Cam started Latin, my relationship with him had changed—*been* changed by my

1

becoming fatherless, in part. In addition to being *fraters*, we were also *puer* (boy) and *deus*.

Cam is short for Cameron. I am Christopher, mostly known as Chris. Our last name is Craven, which no one ever bothered to tell me is a synonym for cowardly, or coward. I learned that from the dictionary at the age of ten. I decided then to change my name when I was old enough to do that—to Christopher de la Chappelle. That sounded awfully good to me; I used to practice writing it. Sometimes I'd put a "Count" in front of it.

I'm seventeen now and so have learned my "Sticks and stones..." and to ask "What's in a name?" I suppose I've come to terms with being a Craven. Of course I've known for years my brother's not a god. But he remains the person I know better and love more than any other.

Today my mother good as told me he's some kind of lunatic and admitted that he's disappeared. She told me the second of these things first, and I hated hearing it, of course. But the first part—that was unacceptable, untrue. How could she believe such nonsense? Or think that I would—ever? She'd have to be crazy herself, which she certainly isn't. She's a little moody, sure, but not crazy, any more than Cam is. We aren't one of those families, believe me. Somebody'd lied to her. That simply had to be the case.

My mother tries to treat me like a kid. I suppose that's standard Mom behavior; I'm what other moms would call her baby, and the only other person living with her in the home she moved into in the year that Cam was born.

And so she didn't tell me all she knew about my brother until she had to.

Six weeks earlier she'd let me know that he'd "temporarily" dropped out of college.

"It's exhaustion," she informed me. "You know how Cammie is, the way he overdoes things. He just needed to rest up—to take it easy for a while."

"He's coming home?" I asked, assuming that.

"No-o," she said. "The people at the college infirmary thought he ought to have a total change, go to a place where he could get away from everything. They recommended Gramercy Manor, in the Berkshires, quite near Tanglewood, I think. It sounds delightful, and ideal for Cam. It's sort of like a yoga center, and sort of like an Outward Bound, and sort of like a writers' colony."

I swallowed all that whole, like liver on a string—that row of "sort of likes," and each an interest of my brother's. And especially that he had worked himself into exhaustion.

As long as I can remember, Cam would get excited about something—some idea or skill—and start to study it, work on it like a madman (oops!), usually for weeks or even months on end. Macrobiotics was his passion for a while; I found it hard to understand how anyone could speak the two words "beans" and "rice" with so much relish. Then he had a magic period. He practiced sleight of hand and juggling for hours every day. His hero at that time was David Copperfield, the TV magic guy, whose act required him to fondle, at some point, his beautiful and barely clad "assistant." Cam was always trying to sign up shapely females at our school, girls who'd put on a bikini and let him practice sawing them in half.

3

"Like a madman" is just an expression, of course; Cam was merely being Cam when he embraced some new excitement. Curious beyond belief, he was a guy who thrived on challenges and liked to push himself. It was not surprising that he'd overdo one time and have to take a break to let his batteries recharge.

I decided I would go and visit him at the Gramercy Manor place as soon as school was over for the year. That'd be my little present to myself, my reward for finishing my junior year without a crippling social or academic misstep, and for being the one who had to stay at home and put up with my mother's moods.

She, Cordelia Craven—mother of Cameron and Christopher, mistress of Charmaine the cat and Cleve the collie dog— had always been emotional. At times she was more fun than anyone, more like an energetic sister than a mom. But even back before my father died, she'd also have her cross and crabby days, which she was apt to treat with vodka tonics. Their effects were not predictable, but never all that good. At best she'd go into her room and stretch out on her chaise, not even bothering to turn on the light. Other times she'd look for faults to find: with food, the house, the weather, local government, and often (how could this be possible?) poor me.

When I first informed her of my plan to visit Cam, she only nodded vaguely and, looking at the kitchen calendar, reminded me about my dentist appointment later on that week. Probably she hoped the dentist would give me some new kind of gas, and I'd get stupid-plan amnesia.

But the third or fourth time that I brought it up, she took a deep, deep breath, then let it out and said we had to talk. As a

4

rule, that meant what we were going to talk about would make my stomach grumble.

"I've been hoping that I wouldn't have to tell you this," she started. "That there wouldn't be a need to. But the fact is that your brother's disappeared."

"Disappeared?" I echoed. "From Gramercy Manor? And he isn't back at college?" Three dumbos in a row, I know, but I was shocked.

"Unfortunately not," she said. "Though college wouldn't necessarily be the right place *for* him at this point. But they looked into that. They had somebody spend some days on campus, speaking to his friends and his professors. There's been no sign of him."

"They?" I said. I didn't like the sound of that at all. "Who's 'they'? The Gramercy Manor people? What—he didn't pay his bill?"

"Probably not," my mother said with just a trace of a smile. "But mainly they—yes, the Gramercy Manor people—were... well, concerned. About how he might be, what he might do."

"Like fall asleep in class at college?" I was doing what I guess I often do when I am forced to hear bad news. I get childish and sarcastic. I suppose I want to kill the messenger. Or at least to wound her with my pull-toy-level wit.

"This Manor," I continued, "could it also be *sort of like* a sanitarium? A high-class loony bin?" What I was doing was taking a worst-case guess and hoping for denial.

Instead my mother flinched a little.

"I don't care for language of that sort," she said. "It isn't funny. Gramercy Manor *is* a private hospital, yes. Cameron was taking medication there. Not just for exhaustion. He was having

5

other problems, which they were trying to treat in a number of different ways."

"You're telling me my brother has some kind of mental illness?" I asked next. "A relative of *mine*? How could a thing like that be possible?"

"I'm not much interested in labels," said my mother, ignoring my buffoonery. "Cam *is*, at times, disturbed—irrational—I'm told. They don't believe he's dangerous to himself or others. And they do believe these episodes of his can be controlled by proper medication. But without it he is…unpredictable. As of now—he disappeared two weeks ago—he's medication-free and out there"—she waved a hand—"wandering around somewhere. By himself, they think. Completely on his own." She heaved another sigh. "Now you know everything that I do."

I sat and stared at her. Clearly she believed my brother was a nut case. Somebody—perhaps some whacked-out college doc—had put that up for sale and she had bought it. I, however, kept my wallet in my pants. Cam could *act* extremely weird, and if you didn't know him the way I did, you might think he had a problem. But I was sure he wasn't crazy, as I've said.

"Well, I know something else that you *don't* know," I told my mother. "When my exams are over, I am going to go and look for Cam. I'll bet you anything I find him—and that there's nothing wrong with him but maybe morning breath and itchy flaking dandruff."

With those announcements and predictions made, I got up and left the room. I didn't want to talk about this…situation anymore just then. I went into my room and stretched out on my bed, not even bothering to turn a light on. If I had a taste for hard liquor, I might have had a vodka tonic first.

6

chapter 2

It would have been okay with me—quite excellent, in fact—if Mom and I had not again discussed my plan to look for Cam.

For one thing, "plan" does my idea a favor. I didn't have a plan other than to go to the last place my brother had been, this Gramercy Manor, and pick up all the information I could get about his stay and his departure.

Because I didn't want to waste time being sensible or logical, I chose to not concern myself with the fact that the people who I imagined supplying me with this information would have acted on it long ago, when the "trail," as they say in old-fashioned sleuthing novels, was still "fresh." No, I just decided my perspective on my brother's unique *style* would allow me to interpret their stale facts and reach conclusions they'd been much too limited to see.

Or maybe I would just get lucky.

Like I'd be walking alone on the grounds of Gramercy Manor and a man with matted hair and a long beard, wrapped in an institutional-gray woolen blanket, would jump out from under a bush and tell me he was John the Baptist, just back from a sojourn in the wilderness, where he'd seen my brother in room 903 at the Holiday Inn in downtown Cleveland, Ohio. And that Cam had said he planned to spend the summer there, where, helped by a computer, he hoped to master *go*, the Japanese board game, as well as throwing cards into a derby hat placed on the floor twelve feet away.

Or perhaps I'd use a restroom at the Manor, and on a square of toilet paper find a note that Cam had written to me: "Chris— If you should happen to unroll this, meet me in the last car of the 4:01 from New York to the Hamptons, any Friday afternoon in August."

But be that as it may, I was unshakable in my determination to go as soon as school was over. And I think my mother realized that short of having people come and glue my naked body to the bathtub, she couldn't stop me. Though she sure did try, by fair means and foul.

Fair: "I want Cam to be safe and...well, let's just say *healthy* quite as much as you do, you know," she said to me one night when we were having dinner. "If I'd thought it would do any good, I would have gone up to Gramercy Manor myself long ago. I've talked to the people up there on the telephone at length. They're the experts in the field, and they don't have a clue about where Cam might be right now."

I didn't like that kind of talk at all. I speared a piece of broccoli and chewed until it liquefied before I answered.

"What do you mean 'experts in the field'?" I asked.

"They're used to people with Cam's problems," said my mother. "They know patterns of behavior."

"Well, I know my own brother's 'patterns of behavior' pretty well myself," I said. "Our relationship is special. I know he'd be expecting me to come and look for him."

I didn't know any such thing, of course. That was more or less a fantasy of mine, a big old piece of wishful thinking.

8

"What they say," my mother said, "is that after a certain period of time, Cam may very well decide he *wants* to come home. At which point he'd give us a call or even just show up. But in the meantime, he could be almost anywhere." She sighed. "I know that doing nothing is hard on you, Chris. How do you think *I* feel? But deep in my heart I do believe it's not just the *only* thing to do—I'm sure it's the right thing, too."

I was looking at her when she said all that, and at one point I was afraid she was going to break down. I hadn't seen my mother cry since that period after my father died, and the truth is I didn't want to see her cry now. That would have been alarming and upsetting, to have her feel that bad. But "deep in my heart I do believe" was right out of a song ("We Shall Overcome") Cam had sung a lot in high school, when his "thing" for a period of months—just before he got into macrobiotics—was the continuing struggle of minorities in this country for social, educational, and economic equality. "We Shall Overcome" was definitely a call to action, in my book.

"Deep in my heart," I told my mother, "I believe that I have to do something other than sit on my duff."

And that was where things stood for a while.

The week before the school year ended we revisited the subject of my search for Cam. And it was then that she tried to use foul play to talk me out of even starting.

"So next Thursday I'll be taking off," I told her. She was in the den watching TV. One of the stations was having a John Wayne festival and she was way out there west of the Pecos, or wherever the Duke was doing his thing. She kept on staring at the screen.

"So where exactly *is* this Gramercy Manor?" I inquired.

The movie broke for a commercial. My mother studied it as if she'd had a Ram-tough truck in mind for her next car.

"I don't think I'm going to tell you." As she said that, Dodge gave way to Mountain Dew.

I wouldn't say I have a very quick temper. Certain things, like bad news or why so few members of Congress will actually vote for meaningful campaign finance reform, *do* make me angry, but as a rule it isn't me who flies into a rage and runs up to his room.

But hearing my mother say that—something as stupid, petty, and childish as that—made me furious.

I picked up a pack of matches from the coffee table and began to light them, one after the other, and toss them, lighted, onto the rug.

"Chris!" my mother yelled. She leaped to her feet and started stamping out my little fires. "Stop that! What do you think you're doing?"

"Copying my mother," I informed her. "Being completely negative and stupid."

"You're just acting crazy," she told me. "Cut it out, will you?"

I'd finished the book of matches by then.

"You know you can't stop me from going," I told her. "So you're just being obstructionist." I'd learned that word in U.S. History class, but I never expected to use it in a sentence, except on an exam.

But what I said was mostly true. I seriously doubt she could have found a judge who'd label me incorrigible or unmanageable and take me into state custody; my mother had no evidence to support such a claim. And thanks to my father, I had my own money—Cam and I both did. Dad had provided it in his will.

It wasn't an inexhaustible amount, but it was much more than enough to feed and clothe me and to keep a car insured and operable.

"Unless you lied to me before, I know it's in the Berkshires and not far from Tanglewood," I said. "How many Gramercy Manors are there going to be in that area? All you'd do by telling me is save me a day or two."

"I suppose," she said. She had sat back down and was now learning what a good neighbor her State Farm insurance agent is.

"All right." She sighed. "I think they even sent a map of how to get there from the turnpike."

"Good," I said. "I know you don't want me doing this, but can't you understand I sort of have to? Can't you see that, Mom?"

She turned around and looked at me.

"I'm starting to," she said. "I could see your father doing what you're going to do. It's probably inherited. You got his 'let's go looking for a needle in a haystack' gene."

I've been told I'm like my dad in other ways as well. Mom says he'd sometimes turn on *Jeopardy* and be just about as well informed as that Alex guy, the host—and *he* had all the answers right in front of him. My dad was something called a systems analyst. I think he was very good at it. He'd tell companies what their electronic needs were. That isn't dangerous work; I don't know why he should have been a cancer victim at the age of thirty-four.

I guess I have Dad's kind of memory and curiosity. I started reading young, at four, and by six or seven I was into the encyclopedia. I wanted an unabridged dictionary for Christmas the year I turned ten. I'm different from Cam, though, in that I don't bury myself in one thing at a time. I like knowing a little something about everything. I guess I was a show-off in my early teens. Other kids would call me Weirdo or Professor.

Picture me: I take up lots of space at six foot four, two thirty—but not prettily, I fear. My mother says that that's intentional, but I can't go along with her. I wouldn't want the sight of me to be offensive to my fellow man—and that goes double for my fellow woman. But admittedly, and depending on your taste, my hair's usually either too long—down over the collar of my shirt because I hate going to the haircut place—or not long enough—because I'm too uncool to even think about a heavy metal look. I wear it parted on one side, it's very straight, dark blond, and there may be weeks that I forget to wash it. A beard is still out of the question, but I don't break out much, either. Neither do I smell. My nose is long and apt to peel in the summertime, and I have a tendency to look down it rather than up or straight ahead. My mother thinks that's both bad manners and a shame, because it means that people often miss my "beautiful blue eyes."

I have big feet, crowded into size thirteens, some flab around my waist, and my posture's not too hot. But I've also got huge hands (that even *I* admire), and though not through any fault of mine, I'm strong. I can twist the top off any jar and have been known to pick up our riding mower and set it on our neighbor's little trailer.

My mother says my size and strength are my inheritance from her grandfather, who was a lumberjack somewhere out West. He used to pull on a two-man saw and swing a double-bitted axe and dance on logs being floated down to the mill. I do none of those things, of course, and very little other exercise, but I'm also light on my feet, the way great-grandpa must have been. Ever since junior high, coaches have suggested that I ought to play their sports. But I am just not interested.

Even on the days I see a letter jacket strolling down a hall at school with someone I desire dripping off him, I am still not interested. Cam said it for the two of us one time: "I just don't go for any sport you have to wear a uniform to play."

Of course I didn't choose to be the way I am, to look and talk the way I do. Nobody does, I guess. They can't. I've read that who we are—how we turn out—is determined by two things: the genetic stuff passed down to us by our parents and the environment in which we grew up. In other words, by "nature" and by "nurture." If that's so, I'm part my father (as I've said) and part my mother—although in what way is less clear to me, other than my size, etc. And because my father died when I was six, my nurturing was done by Mom, and even more so, I would say, by Cam. Being who I am, I was never part of any of the cliques or "types" at school, exactly. I'd always have an odd fair-weather friend or two, people I hung out with for a while. But Cam's the only person whom I trust completely, who totally accepts me. That's just the way it's always been.

chapter 3

Gramercy Manor was a cinch to find. That was due in large part to my mother's map, of course. Because it showed you how to get there from all compass points—not just the turnpike—it covered lots of western Massachusetts, the part that answers to "the Berkshires." I wondered, looking at the thing, if Cam could possibly be camping out up there, in some wild section of that ancient little mountain range.

Yes, it was possible that Cam had "disappeared" into the Berkshires. If so (I thought), I wouldn't stand a chance of finding him. Although, as both my mother and I believed, I'd inherited a lot of how I am from Dad, trackless wilderness was not my kind of haystack. I'm more a streets-and-sidewalks kind of guy. Cam, however, wasn't. Outdoor survival had been huge with him for years. He could start a roaring fire in a cypress bog; he knew which roots and plants were good to eat, not to mention nuts and berries. Give him a jackknife and a fishhook and he'd probably *gain* weight in a wilderness where I would starve to death.

But even if my brother'd soloed off into the woods to hide (from anyone who might be looking for him), he wouldn't plan to stay there. Cam wasn't any hermit crab. He liked and needed people. Before he skipped the Manor he'd have made a master plan. What I had to find up there was someone he had told it to. An informer (friendly witness, undercover agent, "source") was what I needed.

I reached my destination with equal parts of hope and—let's face it—trepidation.

My brother's last-known address turned out *not* to be one spooky building on a hilltop, which is how I sort of had imagined it. What it looked like—yes, I'm guessing now, 'cause no, I've never seen one—was the campus of a snazzy little boarding school. I mean, wouldn't such a place have lush green lawns and big shade trees and speed bumps on the driveway?

And then there were the buildings. First of all, your eyes were drawn to this one central and commanding brick pile with ivy and a big white entranceway; the rest were mostly clapboard painted white or some light color, often with dark shutters. Some were a couple or three stories high, and gabled. Others stretched out sort of like a John Wayne ranch house, only even bigger. Most had spacious porches that held lots of Adirondack chairs and rockers. I assumed the patients sat around on them and schmoozed in their spare time. But I couldn't quite imagine *Cam* doing that—relaxing in a rocking chair and maybe showing card tricks to "Napoleon" or "Jesus."

There was also a big cement block structure next to two all-weather tennis courts: functional and ugly, undoubtedly the gym.

I didn't notice bars on any windows. What I also didn't see were any people. No one was on the porches now or on the benches underneath the trees. No one was walking on the blacktopped paths. I thought to check my watch, and it read 12:48. "Aha," I said to it, "they're all at lunch."

(Lunch is a friend of mine; all food occasions are. I'd left my house at six A.M. after nothing more than English muffins [4]; that'll give you some idea of how anxious I was to get going. But at eleven I decided that it made no sense to fast while looking for my brother, so I stopped and ate three bacon cheeseburgers. I would have ordered still more rapid food except I couldn't get myself to say the two words "biggie fries.")

Next to the brick building was a parking lot with VISITORS on a sign beside it, and I pulled in there. I had my choice of probably a dozen vacant parking spaces, so I picked the one that was farthest from the building. I thought I'd hang out in the car until I saw some signs of life.

It wasn't very long before I did. At 1:01 a steady stream of people began to flow out of the biggest of the ranch houses. Some walked purposefully in groups, others kind of dawdled. As they got closer, I could see that some of them had lots to say while others clearly weren't listening—at least to anyone that anybody else could see. They all appeared to be adults—meaning people who had finished high school or been finished *by* it—and everyone I saw was white. Other than that, they could have been the oncoming pedestrian traffic in a suburban mall—which I realize doesn't say a thing about their sanity, of course. Among the people were half a dozen cheerful-looking dogs.

When the stream got to the big brick building, everybody who wore either a necktie or high heels went up the steps, and disappeared inside. And so did four of the dogs. The rest of the crowd headed right and left toward other buildings.

I got out of my car and followed the better dressers.

This day I was quite well-dressed in a green and red striped rugby shirt, brown Dockers pants, and deck shoes. Wearing that, I could have passed myself off as an inmate of the Manor, although a lot of them were even more informal, settling for sweats and running shoes. I didn't know, of course, how many patients were forbidden belts and had to wear Velcro straps instead of laces on their Reeboks.

Just inside the front door of the building sat a woman at a desk, with a golden retriever lying on a small hooked rug beside her. Both of them looked up when I came in, but neither of them growled or looked alarmed. I imagine that they'd both seen plenty worse come through that door.

"Hello, I'm Christopher Craven," I informed them. "I'm here seeking information—about my brother, Cameron. He was a patient here quite recently."

"Of course," the woman said. I didn't know if that was "Of course he was," or "Of course you are." Because she didn't add to that, I guessed she wanted more from me.

"I was wondering if I could speak to someone who's familiar with my brother's case," I said. I thought that I'd said that already, but you never know what people hear when you are talking. I also thought I might be speaking to a patient near her discharge date who was sitting at that desk as therapy.

She appeared to chew on my request this time. Then she lit up as if she'd had a great idea.

"Let me see if Dr. Bree can see you," she said, getting up.

"Dr. Bree?" I wanted to be sure I'd heard the name right.

"*Brie*," she said again. "Like the cheese. He's our associate director."

"Oh, *Brie*," I parroted. "Just like the cheese: white and soft and salty. But delightful."

The woman smiled uncertainly and headed for a hall that opened off the foyer. The dog got up and followed her.

She wasn't gone for long.

"If you'll just have a seat." She nodded toward two chairs that flanked a table bearing magazines. "Dr. Brie will be right with you."

I went and sat. This reminded me of going to *my* doctor, Dr. Grubb. To him, "right with you" meant the time it took to weigh yourself, steal a tongue depressor and some Q-Tips, wonder if you ought to take your shirt off, and wish about a million times that you were an android. I picked up a copy of *National Geographic*.

But Brie ran on a faster track than Grubb. Before I'd gotten halfway through my search for bare-boobed Polynesian maidens, he was standing next to me.

I lurched onto my feet and took him in. Medium height, fifties probably, short-sleeved white shirt and dark green tie with white lambs grazing on it, a messy bird's nest of graying hair, and teeth that could have put an orthodontist's kid through half a year at Harvard, probably.

He also took me in, and when he had, he said, "Ah—Christopher—*ah*—Craven, is it?"

His tone of voice and *ah-ah* hesitations made me think he wasn't used to people in my age group, and he didn't want to practice on me. That was just the feeling I got. But having said he'd see me, he was stuck. He led me to his office and immediately informed me that my brother'd been a "noncompliant" patient, refusing medication when he could, and uncooperative in other "treatment" programs. Dr. Brie couldn't "*ah*—imagine" where my brother might have disappeared to, and I also got the feeling that he didn't give a flying F about Cam's present health or whereabouts.

"I wonder if there's any chance that someone else—another patient, maybe—might have heard Cam talk about his…plans," I said, grasping at the only straw I had.

"No, *none*," said Brie emphatically—so quickly he forgot to make his trademark sound. Then he slowed back down again.

"Your brother didn't make—*ah*—any effort to be *civil* to one person here," he said. "Much less—*ah*—confide in anyone."

He raised both hands: the "there-you-have-it" gesture—or maybe "I give up"—and stood.

I had to do the same. He walked me to the big front door. I couldn't think of anything to say. As I went down the steps and headed for my car, I realized Dr. Brie and I had never touched.

I also thought that this would be an okay time for John the Baptist to show up.

chapter 4

Did I mention that I'd parked my car right by a patch of empty lawn? Well, now there was a person sitting on that lawn, her back against the left front door of my car. She looked up as I approached.

"You're Chris, Cam Craven's brother," she announced as if I didn't know that.

I stopped before I got too close to her. Face it, she could easily be Joan of Arc—and decide that I was heading to help out with the siege of Orléans.

"Yes," I said. "I am."

"I found that out from Ruth inside," she said, nodding toward the building I had just been in.

"The woman at the reception desk?" I asked. I'd read that some loonies claim that dogs can talk—*have* talked—to them. I mean, "Ruth" *could* have been the dog.

"The very one," this person said, and smiled. She was a great deal younger than Ruth (I'm not so good at guessing females' ages) and was wearing dark blue sweatpants and white running shoes (*with* laces) and a gray T-shirt that had UCLA across the pleasant-looking front of it. She also had a really nice tan and jet black hair, about as straight as mine but longer and parted in the middle and braided. It's hard to tell when someone's sitting down, but she seemed to be quite short, as well as built. Peculiarly, perhaps, I found thinking she could be a crazy made her even more attractive. She had perfect silky-looking skin and big dark eyes.

"I worked with Cam while he was here," she told me, "and I liked him. He's a charming guy."

"Dr. Brie just told me that Cam didn't get along with anybody here," I said. I wondered what she'd meant by what she'd said. Did "worked with" really mean "worked *on*"—or side by side?

"He didn't get along with Dr. Brie," she said. "That's—*ah*—a big mistake if you're a patient."

"And you," I said, "are...?"

I was being slick, I thought. Now she'd have to tell me "on the staff" or (more likely) "someone who had one bad trip too many."

"Michelle Falk," she said elusively. "Cam and I had things in common. That's how come we got along so well. I'm into nature-loving, too. Harmonizing with the earth and treading on it lightly. Surviving in the wilderness. Learning how to be a whole lot less dependent on...all sorts of things. My father's father was a pureblood Mohawk."

"My *great*-grandfather was a lumberjack," I told her. I, too, could drop a pedigree.

"Cam hasn't surfaced yet?" she asked. "Ruth seemed to think he hadn't. That maybe you were looking for him."

"That'd be correct," I said. "I am. He hasn't been in touch with us—my mom and me. Or anybody else, as far as we know."

"If you don't mind my asking this—how come you're looking for him?" she inquired next. "You want to put him back in here—

convince him he should stay this time? Or maybe talk him into someplace else where he could get some help?"

"I don't think so," I replied. I wished she'd said what *she* thought first. "Cam's always seemed okay to me." I had to add to that. "*Better* than okay, in fact. *Much* better. But I guess the people at his college—and some people here—think otherwise. I can't believe they're right, but I'm trying to keep an open mind. I just want to see him, spend a little time with him."

There, I thought. Who could disagree with someone trying to keep an open mind.

Not Michelle Falk, apparently. "That seems reasonable," she said. She looked at her watch. "I have to be somewhere, so I'd better make this quick. Cam may get in touch with me. I think he will. So probably you ought to call me up from time to time. Or were you planning to go home from here? If you were, I could get in touch with you. As soon as I hear something."

She stood up. She was quite short, as I'd suspected, five two or three at best. She had good posture, like a health professional would have, I thought. Of course she still could be a patient, though.

"I'm not exactly sure where I'll be going next," I said. I didn't want to go back home so soon. I hate the two words "summer job" almost as much as "biggie fries." And somehow, even though I hadn't done it very long, I thought looking for my brother suited me.

"So I'd better get in touch with *you*," I said. "But one quick question now before you go. Do *you* think Cam needs help? Belongs in, say, a place like this?" I really wanted to know what she thought. No matter what she was, she'd have an *insight*.

She shook her head. It was the kind of shake that *could* mean

22

"no" but could also mean "you annoy me." She took a good long gander at the ground.

"Those are *two* quick questions," she began as she lifted her head, "which ask for long, slow answers. And I may not be…equipped to give them at the moment."

Then she reached out and put a hand on me—she actually did. Of course she chose a pretty nonerogenous location: my left forearm.

"But call me up, Chris Craven. Promise me you will. I can see that you're a lot like Cam," she said. "Now I *really* have to run."

With that she spun around and actually *did* run. She didn't take a path, but instead loped right straight across the lawn until she reached a light gray clapboard house. I watched her till she disappeared inside.

I'm pretty sure that I was smiling. I don't think I'd ever gotten all that big a compliment before.

chapter 5

I think I kept on standing at that one spot by my car for fifteen minutes, easy. I do that sometimes, kind of freeze. At school I've found myself in classrooms all alone and with the lights turned out—or sometimes it's a custodian who finds me. On those occasions I just never noticed that the class—and sometimes the school day—was over with, and everybody else had left.

This time I was mostly sucking on the memory of what Michelle had said to me, that I was lots like Cam. I've never thought that. She couldn't have been talking about our looks. Cam is three inches shorter than I am and probably seventy pounds lighter. My hair is long, his is short; mine is straight and his is curly. He's actually starting to go bald, not on top but going back from either side of his forehead, while I have follicles to spare. Cam's turned-up nose is the "after" in a plastic surgeon's ad, and his eyes, which come straight at you always, are a golden brown that he calls hazel, very different from my "beautiful blue" pair.

I've often wished my appearance affected people the way Cam's does. There's something about him—maybe it's a certain look in his eyes, or it could be his easy little smile—that makes people comfortable with him as soon as they meet him. My looks can put some people off, but Cam is universally accessible.

So if it wasn't looks, then what? Might she have thought I was a "charming guy," like Cam? *Extremely* dubious. Unlike me, Cam is never ill at ease around people, never at a loss for words. When he goes into a store, he often ends up having a little conversation with the salesclerk in which it turns out the two of them have things in common—like a taste in music, clothing, or food. You could tell strangers really hoped Cam would "have a nice day" when they said that to him.

Of course, Michelle, being part Native American, *could* be unusually perceptive and tuned into stuff, including people's natures, their real—though hidden—selves. Perhaps (I told myself) her keen eyes cut right through my slightly awkward, not-so-hot exterior and reached my fragrant center: my witty, gentle, thoughtful...soul. (That's probably something of a poetic exaggeration, but I guess I do feel I'm basically nice, if not exactly "charming." I believe I've got a lot of love to offer someone, but maybe everybody feels that way.)

And oh, sure—there also are a couple of little ways Cam and I are completely similar. Neither of us likes to ride on rollercoasters (though he can laugh about his fears and call himself a scaredy cat). And we both are very good at tongue twisters (particularly the one that starts "Theophilus Thistle, the successful thistlesifter, while sifting a fistful of unsifted thistles...").

But I doubt that even a member of the Mohawk tribe of the Iroquois Confederacy could possibly have guessed those two.

I refused to even consider (seriously) that Michelle believed I was a lot like Cam in that I, too, needed "help." I hadn't said anything weird to her. And, of course, I didn't even know if she was trained to make that kind of judgment. It was possible she'd had to run over to that gray building because she was late for some therapy appointment—for getting it, not giving it. But I didn't really want to think that.

She had run awfully gracefully. Watching her had been a treat. I'd seen she did tread lightly on the earth, just the way she said.

After a while I shook myself and thought I ought to move from off that spot. But should I leave the campus right away, I wondered? If I stuck around...who knows? I might, for instance, meet the guy who'd cleaned my brother's room the day he skipped...which meant he'd also emptied Cam's wastebasket...in which he'd found...let's see...a Greyhound bus schedule that had a certain destination starred and circled....Not bloody likely, that, but hey, people win the lottery. You never know.

I turned around just then and glanced back at the big brick building I had recently come out of. And there, standing by his office window, was that cheesy Dr. Brie. He was looking out, right in my direction, and talking (urgently, it seemed to me) into a cellular telephone.

Believe me, I got right into my car and started it and, bouncing on the speed bumps, scooted down the driveway.

Once I got on to the highway I was faced with this: I'd told my mother I was going to find my brother and I hadn't. Nor had I found some person at the Manor who both knew and chose to share Cam's "master plan." I was looking like an idiot, a bull-shitter, a cockeyed optimist, a failure—and worst of all, a *kid*, clueless and without a further plan. I didn't even know where I was going.

So rather than keep going, I pulled right off the highway the first chance I got. "Scenic View," the sign had said. I slid into a parking space beside a low stone wall and closed my eyes. It wasn't the scenery I needed, but ideas. Good ideas—some hope. There had to be some smart things even I could plan to do.

While I was waiting for an inspiration, my mind took off and wandered back to that Michelle again. That was typical of me: to think about a girl I'd never get. But she had obviously liked me; that was something, anyway. I decided then and there that I would call her—and every couple of days. He might call her any time—tonight, for instance. And she had said she'd pass on to me anything she heard from him. She was my best— let's face it, only—contact/lead. I definitely was going to stay in touch with her.

And then—imagine this huge light bulb going on above my head—I thought of Lisa Reston and Allen York. They were, in order, Cam's most recent girlfriend and his college roommate.

And they also were two other people Cam might get in touch with—as well as people who could tell me how he'd acted (also anything he'd said) just before he went (got carted off?) to Dr. Brie's exclusive funny farm.

So what I had to do right now (I told myself delightedly) was call up Mom and get her to look in Cam's at-home address book by the phone and read me off the home addresses of that pair, plus their phone numbers.

Yes—oh, yes! There were other places I should go (right now!) and people I should see. Finding Cam would not be quite as easy as I'd made it sound when talking to my mom. It was clearly going to take some time and effort. This was not a sim- ple matter, not by any means. I had to be prepared to run down many leads and reach discouraging dead ends. But I would also have to always keep on going, never close the file, use up as much shoe leather (or, hopefully, tire tread) as it took. I could pray for further inspiration but expect that good old-fashioned perspiration, in the end, would be what cracked the case. Inspector Craven, Scotland Yard, was about to put his long nose on what little scent there was, determined to pick up his missing brother's trail.

Revitalized, I started up the car again and drove on down the road. Aha! Ahead was Rosie's Quik Stop. No cars were outside it; I wouldn't have to wait to use the phone.

My mother's mood was excellent, apparently.

"Sure," she chirped when asked if she'd accept the charges on a call from Chris. "Most gladly. Absotively. Posilutely."

I told her I'd made a good start at the Manor and had even found someone who might lead me to Cam eventually. And that meanwhile there were "other avenues I wanted to explore."

When I told her what—or actually *who*—those other avenues were, she was relieved, I think. It's perfectly possible that one of the reasons my mother hadn't wanted me to go off looking for Cam was that having had one son "disappear," she was worried that the other one might, too. Allen and Lisa were both known quantities; they wouldn't let her "baby" get in any trouble.

So pretty soon I was scribbling addresses and phone numbers on the back of the Gramercy Manor map. It wasn't easy writing with a cheap ballpoint pen on paper held up against the metal side of a mini phone booth. The pen stopped writing all the time, and what I had to do was…never mind. I got the information down. And Mom was so pleasant and easy to deal with that I promised I'd get back to her again in a couple of days.

After I hung up, I wondered if my mother's mood was the result of Cam's having showed up at the house shortly after I left—just as the "experts" said he might. Maybe he was there now, and Mom was keeping him all to herself while she figured out what to do about him next. I know she feels I complicate things—such as her life—sometimes.

Well, that was a chance I had to take. By that time it was four P.M. and I'd had a long day already. I decided what I ought to do was drive an hour or so away from the Berkshires. That'd mean I'd gotten started on Step Two. I'd put up at a motel. I could then make my next set of calls from the comfort and privacy of a room of my own. One that had a pool outside, perhaps, and cable, posilutely.

chapter 6

I had to fight off a strong desire to register under an alias when I checked in at the Valley Vue Motel. I guess I don't like to leave footprints where I've been if I can help it; I'd never realized that about myself before. But, I mean, suppose you put down your right name and address on a motel registration card, for instance. What's to prevent the motel owner from writing your mother after you check out?

"Dear Mrs. Craven," they could say, "we imagine you'd like to know that your son Chris left the bathroom in our unit 12 a total mess: towels not hung up neatly, washcloth in a sodden ball, etc. He also helped himself to all the matches, notepaper, soaps, and cosmetics—even the sewing kit and shoeshine rag— we lay out in the rooms for our guests' convenience, should they forget to bring their own. Are you going to tell me that this great ox of a boy uses both bath oil and a shower cap? We hope you'll have a talk with him as soon as he..." etc., etc., etc.

I'm not saying that *would* happen, but it could. It's within the realm of possibility. Inspector Craven, returning to his home sweet home, could do without that kind of bitter aftertaste.

It took me a few minutes after I entered unit 12 to psyche myself up to use the phone. Having the *idea* to call up Lisa Reston

30

and Allen York was one thing. Actually making the calls, bringing those two conversations to successful fruition, was another thing altogether. Ideas are all well and good, but better in some situations than others. I imagine if you're an "idea man" at some big company like IBM or AT&T, you're assigned a bunch of stooges whose job it is to convert your brilliant thoughts into workable action. The nice thing about that is *you* get the big money and the lion's share of the credit, and *they* get headaches and self-doubt, stress-related injuries, and personality disorders leading to divorce. Another good thing about being an "idea man" in business and industry is that I don't think you have to work your way up into the job. I think you can be one of those right out of college, just about. That sounds like something I could go for: having people say I was a wunderkind. That'd be cool.

Anyway, the trouble with putting my idea about calling Lisa and Allen into action was that, fantasies aside, I wasn't actually *friends* with either of the people I planned to call and later go to see. I knew them only in the sense of having met each of them a few times, always in or near my house or on the college campus.

"You remember my 'little' brother Chris," Cam might say after I blundered into the kitchen while he and one of them were pressure-cooking rice. And whoever it was would probably say, "Little. Right." Followed by a "Sure. Hi, Chris."

Or if I came back from a mall and Cam and the other one were throwing a Frisbee out on the lawn, we might have one of those scintillating conversations that take place when someone asks a kid like me "How's school?"

But still, this wasn't any time to fret about whatever either of them thought of *me*. Cam was the subject here, and, well, my urgency would be quite understandable. Mine and my mother's,

31

that is. I planned to tell both of them that I was speaking on our two behalves.

I began by dialing Lisa Reston's number.

In truth, I had sort of a crush on Lisa. (I say "sort of a crush" to keep from saying "the mother of all crushes," you should understand.) On one level I knew that it was ridiculous and pointless—she was older, cooler, gorgeous, and liked Cam. I'd be just a kid to her. Yet when she was twenty-eight, I'd be all of twenty-four, a kid no more. Conceivably, by then a wunderkind. So how might that play out? In my fantasy I'd have kept in touch with her through all the years, and (this was essential to my plan) at some point she'd been dumped by Cam. Then, one afternoon at my estate in Malibu, I'd be stretched out beside my question-mark-shaped pool, working on another great idea (that over time would change the lives of every person on the planet) and there she'd be, coming out of the cabana, walking toward me with a towel around her neck and nothing more on anywhere.

Of course, she wasn't home right then. The one who answered was her younger brother Lenny, who, going by the way he sounded, was even more of a kid than I am. But he tried to be extremely helpful once he'd heard I was Cam Craven's brother. He thought Cam was "a super guy."

Naturally, I knew that Lisa was an aspiring vocalist, so it was no surprise to me to learn she'd recently hooked up with Wholly Frail, which was (so Lenny said) "a really up-and-coming all-girl band." For the next three days, he told me, the band would be appearing at a club somewhere around Newport, Rhode Island. The name of the club (he sniggered as he said this) was Wrong Island Sounds Saloon, and he didn't have a phone number for it, or know where Lisa might be staying or even where the band was heading when this gig was over with.

While all of that was not the best of news, neither was it all that bad. Newport, Rhode Island, was just a hop, skip, and jump—or a few tacks if you're sailing, I suppose—from Allen York's parents' place on the Connecticut shore. It, in turn, was less than half a tank of gas away from where I was right then, near the Massachusetts border. All I had to do was pray Cam's roomie was at home.

God was alert and merciful. Allen was in residence—and friendly, welcoming, and most concerned about my brother. He asked me to come down and have a "bite of lunch" with him, the next day.

chapter 7

"Still no word from Cam?" was how he greeted me as I was getting out of my car.

He'd been sitting on the porch of his parents' house when I pulled in to their little driveway. The house was an upscale-home-in-a-Connecticut-village model: white with green shutters, big, two-storied, cedar-shingled roof, ancient maple trees out front, wind chimes tinkling discreetly.

Cam had told me Allen planned to be a teacher. He was a slightly built, baby-faced blond person with a mild and friendly manner. I could see him at a blackboard showing people how to do quadratics—and later giving them a lot of partial credit on their tests.

"Not a peep, I'm sorry to say," I answered.

We shook hands and I let him lead me into the house and through it to a spacious country kitchen.

The "bite of lunch" he'd offered me turned out to be a veritable feast. From the big double-door refrigerator he pulled packages of deli-wrapped cold meats and cheese, a covered container of egg salad, and jars of pickles, mayonnaise, and mustard. Out of a cabinet came loaves of sour rye and whole wheat bread, a half-dozen bakery hard rolls and a giant bag of crinkle-cut potato chips.

"For sandwiches," he told me, nodding at the food. "If you'll just help yourself…"

"Thank you. Sure," I told him. "Everything looks great." I was reminded of the thought I'd had the day before, that looking for my brother suited me just fine.

"I really appreciate your seeing me," I added, already into smearing country-style mustard onto two slices of rye bread, then adding thick layers of rosy-pink baked ham and holey, fragrant Swiss.

"Hey, more than happy to," he answered. He'd gotten himself a bowl and a box of Cheerios. Apparently he hadn't had his breakfast yet.

"What my mom and I were wondering," I said, "is how Cam was when you last saw him, and particularly whether he said or did anything that might help us figure out where he might have gone to now."

After a bit of a struggle, Allen had managed to open both the box and the sealed wax-paper package that the Cheerios were in. Now he filled his bowl half full of them and picked up a banana from the counter behind him. He looked at it as if he'd never had one in his hands before, I thought.

"Cam surely didn't like it at the Manor," he said, looking not at me but at the banana as if it was unrecognizable. "He said they tried to treat him like a two-year-old—telling him to drink his milk and practice finger-painting."

Suddenly he seemed to know exactly what to do. Making quick, decisive movements, he peeled and sliced the banana like a breakfast pro.

I, of course, was looking at him bug-eyed.

"Wait," I said. "You saw Cam *after* he took off from there? He made a stop at the college?"

35

"Yeah, and he looked great," said Allen, smiling at the contents of his bowl. "He didn't stay long, though."

"So what did he say?" I asked excitedly. "Did he act—you know—*all right*? Did he tell you what his plans were?" Without even thinking about what I was doing, I spread mayonnaise on both halves of a hard roll, mounded roast beef on one half, and salted and peppered it.

"He didn't talk about his future plans at all," said Allen. "He acted sort of secretive, in fact. But otherwise he seemed, like, normal. He looked well rested, and he'd put a lot of weight back on."

I stared at him. There really wasn't room on my plate for potato chips, so I just rested the open bag against the mustard jar right next to it. I wasn't hogging them—no one eats potato chips with Cheerios.

I took a big bite of my ham and cheese sandwich while I thought about what Allen had just said. The ham was sweet and smoky, the cheese mild and nutty, and the mustard added spice to all those flavors.

"This is all so good." I waved the sandwich at Allen. "But do you happen to have anything cold to drink? Like a soda?"

"Oh, sure," he said. He went right over to the fridge again. "There's seltzer, ginger ale, some open tonic water, Pepsi…"

"Pepsi would be great," I said, and he pulled out two cans and set them down in front of me. Then he turned back and got out a quart of milk. I popped a top and took a swig.

"Did you just say he put a lot of weight *back on*?" I asked, getting back to…well, you might say, business. "Had Cam been sick before he left, or something?"

Allen poured some milk into his bowl.

"Uh-yah, you might say that," he said. "He'd been doing

36

some strange shit, but you know Cam. You know how he gets into stuff and sort of goes and goes with it."

"Indeed I do," I said. "What was it this time?" I picked up my roast beef sandwich and bit into it. Fantastic.

"It was…I guess you'd say a *cat* thing," Allen said. "And it took a lot of practice, right from the beginning."

"*Practish?*" I asked through a big mouthful.

"Right. First he got this cat from the humane society and started studying it…"

"*Studying* it?" I said. I hate it when my mom does that: repeats some word I just said, but makes a question out of it. But I couldn't seem to help myself.

"What Cam set out to do," said Allen, speaking slowly and patiently, as if I were a class of really slow learners, "was to live exactly like a cat—see how catlike he, a person, could become. He changed his life around completely. Instead of sleeping nights he took catnaps during the day. Every time he'd wake up he'd do a lot of stretching, the way a cat does—and I must say he got really limber doing that. Then he'd pussyfoot around—practice walking noiselessly. Nights, he'd go outside and hunt."

"You're kidding me," I said. I was eating fast, taking quick hits on my sandwiches, or a handful of chips, and washing down each mouthful with a swig of soda.

"Absolutely not," said Allen. "Although that doesn't mean he went and killed a bunch of mice and birds and ate them raw." He laughed at the absurdity of that, then paused and seemed to think things over. "At least I don't believe he did. I think he practiced creeping up on what he called his 'quarries.' Most of them were *things*, actually, like the sculptures they have all over

37

campus, or a bench, or a parked car. But every now and then he'd stalk a dog he found tied up outside the library. Or maybe someone—I mean, a *couple*—making out." He shook his head and chuckled.

"God," I said, not liking this at all. My brother practicing sneaking up on *parked cars*? "How long did that go on?"

"Weeks," said Allen. "Weeks and weeks. That's how come he got burned out. He wasn't getting proper sleep or even eating right—he lived on canned tuna and Grape-Nuts. He tried to tell me that the little rocky stuff was cat chow, but I tried some once and I swear it was Grape-Nuts. Cam claimed his diet helped him see a whole lot better in the dark."

I took a piece of whole wheat bread and spread egg salad on it. Creeping up on parked cars? Eating tuna fish and Grape-Nuts? What did it all mean? Was this just Cam being Cam or was it…well, a little *too* far out?

Allen wasn't acting all that shocked by what he'd said. He was gobbling his breakfast now, eating spoonful after spoonful as fast as he could go.

I thought of something else to ask him.

"How come the college docs got on Cam's case?" I said. "Did he go in for help?"

"No, no, indeed," said Allen, putting down his spoon. "What happened was, this one morning Lisa found him curled up on her doormat in the rain. He was breathing funny and he looked like hell, and when she couldn't get him to stand up and come inside, she called an ambulance. She was afraid he might have taken something—an overdose of catnip, possibly. That was part of how come he ended up in Gramercy Manor, that one incident."

"*Part* of how come?" I repeated. I started on the second Pepsi.

"When the people at the college infirmary started asking around," Allen said, "they discovered Cam had been blowing off most of his classes and wasn't handing in much work. I also may have mentioned the cat business to them—just for Cam's sake. I tried to tell them Cammie always waited till the end of a term—about the last two weeks—before he started working, and that he still made A's and B's. I guess I didn't want to...well, admit that he was acting...differently."

He looked away from me when he said that, then got up and poured a cup of Mr. Coffee's preparation.

"So what you *do* think, Allen," I began, sounding like Inspector Craven and pointing at him with what I had in my hand, which happened to be a potato chip, "is that last term, Cam, my brother, wasn't acting 'normally.'" I ate the chip and, to express quotation marks, held up the first two fingers of each hand.

He came back to the table and sat down again.

"I guess I *do* think that," he said. "And I know Lisa did, too. He was still Cam, but even more so, if you know what I mean. Not all the time, maybe, but some of it."

I nodded, looking at my plate. There was just a bite or two left of my sandwiches, and I felt about the way they looked: worked over. Sure, I'd learned some things, but not exactly *nice* things, and nothing that'd help me find my brother.

It seemed that Allen could read my mind.

"I'm sorry, Chris," he said. "I know I haven't been much help. I can't imagine where Cam's got to. Maybe he's called Lisa, but I kind of doubt it. He got pretty mad at her. For calling the ambulance that day."

39

Fine, I thought—another piece of irrational behavior by my brother. Suddenly I wanted to be done with Allen York and with this conversation, before he thought of something else I didn't want to hear.

"Well," I said, babbling the lines that any boob in my position would probably come up with, "if you hear anything or think of anything, you've got our number, right? My mom and I would sure appreciate a call." Having said that, I stood up.

"Sure," said Allen, "absolutely." I could tell that he was feeling bad, apologetic—guilty.

"How about an ice cream bar for the road?" he asked me.

I took one, partly so he'd feel a little better, and he walked me to my car. But when we got to it, he did a double take.

"Hold on," he said. "This should have registered before—it's just that I was half-asleep, I guess. But—Cam had a car like this the day he came to school. What is this anyway, a Honda? This is what he had—I'm sure of it. A white Honda, same as this, four doors. But his"—he bent his head and closed his eyes—"his had New York plates. Yes, and a Ben and Jerry's bumper sticker."

chapter 8

The ice cream bar was not my favorite kind.

I guess I'm a purist when it comes to frozen dessert on a stick. The simplest is the best: rich, creamy vanilla ice cream covered by a crisp and uniform layer of dark, semisweet chocolate. Just don't make the mistake of eating one of those with a white cotton shirt on, though. Five times out of ten a sizable piece of that chocolate coating will drop off onto your shirt and start to melt before you get it off. Co-ed Naked Dove Bar Eating (which I haven't yet seen on a T-shirt) could be quite delightful, though.

(In the lesser world of Popsicles—frozen flavored water on a stick—I prefer raspberry to the more popular orange. But Popsicles aren't trouble-free, either. Experience suggests that if you want to break a double Popsicle into two singles, you shouldn't try to do it by twisting the sticks. You'd think the god of sharing would watch over this, but no. More often than not, one will break, and a big chunk of it will fall on [hopefully] the ground, there to be devoured by a passing dog.)

Anyway, the ice cream bar that Allen gave me had cookie crumbs all over it and two flavors of ice cream inside. That kind of bar is trying just a little bit too hard, in my opinion.

Now, having just gone on and on about ice cream bars, I sort of want to take it all back. I probably shouldn't mention food so much. I wouldn't want to give a wrong impression—about my priorities and everything. Sure, eating is just about my main pleasure, and I do eat a lot, but it simply isn't true that my interest in food, at this point in my life, is anything like my interest in finding my brother and taking care of him. (And I'm pretty sure that if I had a girlfriend I'd be more interested in her than in food. I read somewhere that for some people eating lots is more or less a substitute for sex.)

It isn't that I'm convinced Cam needs "taking care of," I should hasten to add. I still basically believe that he was sent to Gramercy Manor as a result of a big misunderstanding. And that if the college doctors had taken the trouble to look into his past history a little more thoroughly, they might very well have realized that the things he was doing (and not doing) on campus were pretty close to SOP—standard operating procedure—for him. That cat business was a little...unusual, granted, but Cam had never been one to specialize in "the usual." It was possible that experimenting with a cat's diet had been his big mistake. Without realizing it, he could have weakened himself to the point he more or less passed out on his girlfriend's doorstep. I mean, tuna and Grape-Nuts wouldn't keep *my* strength up, I can guarantee you that. When you don't eat right, it's easy to come down with something.

So perhaps...and then suddenly it came to me: the explanation for...well, *everything!*

Cam wasn't just weak from a bad diet. He'd probably picked up some exotic *virus!*

I knew a lot of exchange students were at his college; chances are that one of them had brought along a bug from some faraway land, a bug that didn't even have a name yet. A virus, and the fever that went with it, could cause all sorts of unusual behavior. Whatever "sickness" Dr. Brie perceived in Cam was doubtless *physical*, not mental. And when the bug finally wore off and went away, and Cam became himself again and found that he was being treated like a two-year-old in a high-class loony bin, he did what anyone would do in his shoes: he bugged on out of there!

I was clearly headed in the right direction now. Lisa would have noticed what was going on with Cam. She would have seen him getting worse and worse as the virus took hold. Guys don't really notice health things, but women do. She'd probably been worrying for weeks before the day she called that ambulance; chances are she'd begged him to go to the infirmary and see a doctor. Maybe she even took his temperature a time or two.

Now I had a third good thing to add to the two pieces of positive information I'd picked up at Allen York's: that Cam was looking/feeling fine after he got out of the Manor and that he was driving a white Honda (with New York plates and a Ben & Jerry's bumper sticker). How he'd come by the car I didn't know, and almost didn't care. I couldn't wait to get to Newport, and the Wrong Island Sounds Saloon.

It took a little doing—I got lost in Newport and had to ask directions from three different people—but I finally found the place at five P.M. It wasn't any hotbed of activity when I walked into it.

What I was looking at was a big room with a bandstand at one end of it. At the other end, and also partway along one of

43

the sides, was the longest bar I'd ever seen, with stools enough for thirty people, easy. Only three were occupied just then, however, way down at one end. Two guys with long-necked beers looked like construction workers (boots and jeans and muscle T's, great tans); one stool away from them was someone in a cowboy hat who was staring at a stubby glass he had both hands around.

A sizable floor fan was stirring up the air and letting out a steady hum. A young-looking balding fat guy was using a push broom around the tables that surrounded the minimal dance floor; all the tables had chairs turned upside down on them. He didn't seem that into hygiene. The place smelled perfect, to my way of thinking, an adult mix of beer and cigarette smoke.

The bartender was down by the two tanned guys, watching TV. I'm pretty sure it was *Baywatch*; he had the sound turned off. He could have been the older brother of the push-broom guy.

I slid part of my butt onto a stool two down from Cowboy Hat.

The bartender looked over. He didn't take a step toward me, nor did he say "Good afternoon" or "What's your pleasure?" Instead he made a tiny movement with his head that I interpreted to mean "Don't try to kid me, kid. I know you're underage. So...what?"

"A Coke," I said, "and hopefully a little information."

Cowboy Hat and the other two guys all turned their head in my direction. I realized I'd probably sounded like a kid trying to sound like a PI, or someone in a prime-time cop show. My "inspector" voice was not perfected yet.

The bartender squirted cola into a glass out of something that looked like what my mother rinses dishes with.

"Ninety-five," he said as he set the glass down in front of me. You'd think I would have gotten ice for that kind of money.

"I'm a friend of someone in the show," I said, "one of them in Wholly Frail. I need to get in touch with her." I'd practiced those lines in my head. I put a dollar on the bar.

"Oh, yeah?" He sounded bored. "Which one?"

"Lisa," I replied. "The singer." At least I knew it wasn't cool to use last names.

"There's lotsa guys'd like to get in touch with *her*," he told me, pocketing my dollar bill. "But what the girls say is they don't got any 'friends.' Or put it this way—that their real friends already know how to get in touch with them."

"Well, the thing is," I informed him, "this is kind of unexpected. She didn't know that I'd be coming here. I didn't know myself till yesterday. Something came up. And now I need to see her pretty bad. It's...well, about her boyfriend."

"Oh—her *boyfriend*," said the guy. I smiled and nodded. "In that case you can see her," he went on, "at showtime."

"What?" I said.

"You come and watch the show and you can see her, just like everybody else."

"You're saying you won't tell me how to reach her now?" I asked.

"*Bingo!*" said the guy, and shot me with his forefinger.

"And showtime is what time?"

"Could be nine," he said, "or ten. Anywhere in there." He walked away on that.

When he got back to where he'd been before, he squirted half a glass of something for himself. All that friendly chitchat must have dried his throat, I figured. As he sipped, he got back

45

to watching TV T&A again. I decided that I wouldn't ask about my change.

What I did at that point was drive back to a deli I'd passed and get a bunch of food I could eat in the car while Inspector Me conducted a stakeout of Wrong Island Sounds. At some point, I figured, Lisa and the rest of Wholly Frail would have to show. The food wasn't any big deal: a couple of subs on Italian bread, barbecue-flavored chips, and a box of chocolate-frosted cupcakes. To drink, a two-liter bottle of Mountain Dew, for the caffeine.

The girls pulled in at twenty after eight. Even before anyone got out of the van, I told myself, "It's them." I just had a feeling. The four of them and I all left our vehicles at the same time and headed for the club, me following.

"Lisa?" I called out when I got close. By then I'd recognized her silhouette: the pixie haircut, her long, sharp nose, that free and easy stride. She had on baggy clothes that hid her other assets, and a big bag swung from her right shoulder.

All four stopped and turned around.

"It's Chris Craven," I went on, and when no one answered right away, I added "Cam's little brother." I threw a nervous laugh in there.

"Oh, yeah—*Chris*," she said. "Surprise, surprise. I can't say I expected you." Her voice did not jump up and down for joy.

"I know, I know," I said. "If I could've called ahead, I would've. I tried to get you at your house. Your brother Larry told me where you were. He didn't have a number I could call, though."

"Lenny," Lisa said. "Not Larry, *Lenny*."

"What?" I said. "Oh, Lenny—*right*." I slapped myself upside the head. "But look, I need to talk to you. About Cam. He's *disappeared*, you see. Would there be any time…?" Even as I spoke I felt impatience setting in, at least on the part of the band-mates.

Lisa looked at them; she looked at me; she flapped her arms, just one time, quickly, up and down.

"We're sort of in a rush," she said. "And later won't be any good because—" She cut that off. "Tell you what—come with us right now. I can talk to you a little bit while I'm getting dressed." It sounded like she sighed.

The others seemed okay with that. Or at least they turned and started for the club. I hustled to keep up.

"No, I can't recall him coming down with anything or even saying he felt bad," she said. "Of course I didn't see that much of him the last few weeks he was at school."

She'd taken off the dark blue oversize and long-sleeved top that she'd been wearing and was sitting there in a light blue work shirt, leaning toward the mirror in the act of putting makeup on.

"I wouldn't say he even *acted* sick, not physically, anyway— unless you want to count the way he *talked*. That sure was weird. And then one day—I hadn't seen him for more than a week— there he was, totally collapsed on my doorstep. I don't know if you heard about that or not."

When we'd gone into the dressing room, which would have been about the right size for one person, never mind four, she'd put me in a chair with my back to the other three. The feeling that I'd had outside got worse, like I was being *tolerated*, barely.

"Yes," I said, "I guess I did. If you mean the time you called the ambulance. Allen mentioned that to me today. Allen York."

She wrinkled up her nose. She hadn't even asked about Cam's disappearance—like, is your *mother* awfully worried?

"Allen—yeah. I'm sure he told you Cam despised my doing that," she said. "My maybe saving his life. I don't know what I was *meant* to do. Just let him lie there? Come *on*. It wasn't only that he couldn't stand, he couldn't even *speak*. He looked like he'd OD'd on something." She stood up and undid the drawstring at the waist of her floppy-legged gray trousers.

I decided maybe I should change the subject. She obviously wasn't going along with my virus theory. At all. She'd blown it off completely. Now all that was left for me to do was fish for any other information she might have.

"Before, you said that he was talking weird," I said. "Could you tell me in what way? What kinds of things he said?" She still might give me clues about Cam's destination.

"Oh, sure," she said. She let her pants drop to the floor and stepped away from them. She had on the kind of underpants that don't have any real back—a thong, I'm pretty sure they're called. I made it a point to keep my eyes up—on the side of her head—in case she turned around.

"Oh, absolutely." She was sounding more sarcastic. "Did you know that the latest number one on Cammie's charts was the Australian Aborigines?" She shook a pair of shiny black pants out of her giant shoulder bag and proceeded to wriggle into them. It took a little doing—there wasn't any slack in there. Under pants like those, her underpants made sense.

48

"He said he had to go and study tracking with them," Lisa told me. "But not in person, no. He believed he could do that in his dreams and through the visions that he'd have when he was fasting. That was part of what he planned to do this summer: dream, go on some extended fasts, and have these visions. He was pissed I didn't want to do that too."

This, of course, was altogether new material. Neither Allen nor Michelle had mentioned Aborigines, or dreams, or fasts, or visions. Lisa was making Cam, my brother, her old boyfriend, sound completely cuckoo.

Stunned, I gave my head a little shake. "That does sound pretty weird, all right," I said. "He couldn't have been kidding, could he? Allen didn't mention stuff like that at all. He talked about Cam living like a cat."

Lisa waved a hand. Then she unbuttoned her shirt, took it off, and replaced it with a ruffled white silky number that had big wide sleeves and buttoned at the wrists. She wasn't wearing any bra or undershirt or anything. She didn't seem to care how much of her I saw unclothed.

"Oh, right," she said. "His cat thing. That was something else. But all this stuff was linked to all the rest of it—maybe not in other people's minds, but in his own, for sure. He said it had to do with Proper Being, which in turn would lead to Proper Living. It wasn't just survival he was interested in; it was survival *plus*."

She rolled her eyes around. "Your brother Cam," she said, "was anxious to create—'perfect,' he said—a new relationship between God and man and nature, in which each one was seen as part and parcel of the other. Like an 'undivided trinity,' he said. To do this he—and others, he hoped—had to return to how people were before they got stacked up in cities and involved with all the things that dulled their senses, took away their hardiness, and organized them to the point that they stopped thinking and feeling for themselves." She took a deep breath.

"But to me," she said, "it sounded like he was trying to pretend that progress hadn't happened, that the last three thousand years or whatever it is of civilization were a total waste of time. It seemed like he wanted to waltz right back into Adam and Eve country, or close to it."

She didn't sound angry as she recited all this. She sounded basically fed up. As if she was sick and tired of thinking about and talking about my brother and his theories or beliefs. Now she was baring her teeth at the mirror, checking for lipstick on them, I suppose.

I could only assume that what she'd just said was somewhat related to what Michelle had talked about—how she, like Cam, was into nature-loving and treading lightly on the earth and all that. But Lisa had put a different spin on it, a nasty kind of spin, as if it were a lot of craziness.

All at once I went from being stunned to *hating* what was happening. This stop now seemed like a disaster. Lisa, longtime centerpiece of many of my fantasies, had offhandedly undressed in front of me—as if I were a sexless creature of some sort, a neutered Saint Bernard, perhaps. (Probably, uncaringly behind my back, the other members of the band had gotten naked, too. I'd heard some silk-on-silk-type sounds.) But Lisa'd also showed me *another* side of herself, a mean, vindictive, twisted side. So Cam had back-to-nature thoughts and theories— don't a lot of people? What made him so different from Thoreau, the *Walden* guy?

I rifled through the contents of my mind, searching for an

explanation for her...well, nastiness, her total lack of understanding and...well, compassion. And I found one: Cam had dumped her. "Hell hath no fury like a woman scorned" was a quote, a warning, that my mother'd taught me. Cam had probably developed an interest in Native people, worldwide—the Australian Aborigines and the Mohawks and so on. And she couldn't share that interest, so he dumped her. It was actually neat that he wanted to pull everything together and study man's spiritual side along with the physical side and the environment. For sure, that was a whole lot better way to spend one's time than...oh, say, singing with a rock 'n' roll band!

There wasn't any conflict of interest here for me. My brother was a curious, vital, interesting person, and Lisa Reston was an angry, shallow bitch. Nice looking? Oh, I guess. But so are a lot of people.

"So you basically have no idea where Cam might be right now," I said coolly, getting to my feet. She hadn't said any such thing, of course, but I felt that I was safe in assuming that. And I really didn't want to hear any more of her wild distortions of my brother's thoughts and theories. Now that I was standing up, I couldn't help noticing that the other three girls had gotten into boots and skintight minis. "Or where he might be heading."

"No idea," she said, and shrugged. "And not the slightest interest."

Outside I made what I believe was a mature—indeed, percipient—decision: I wouldn't hang around to watch the show. If the band was any good, I reasoned, it wouldn't be doing a gig where it was stuck in such a lousy little dressing room.

chapter 9

Back in my car I contemplated driving home. It was hardly an attractive prospect—not the drive itself so much as getting there and talking to my mother.

She'd hear me coming in, and dollars to doughnuts, she'd get up and put on her bathrobe, come downstairs, and say, "So tell me all about it..." with that "wise" look on her face.

I can't stand that bathrobe of my mother's, to tell you the truth. It looks a little like an old-fashioned flannel nightshirt, except with big white buttons up the front. I don't know if she thinks it's cute, or what. *I* think it's time she headed in a new direction, bathrobe-wise.

So I drove down the coast for maybe thirty miles and put up in a room at the Harbor View Motel. It had little anchors on its matches, soap, and towels; they all were safe from me.

The following morning I sort of picked at my breakfast (OJ, coffee, scrambled eggs with sausage and home fries, a side order of waffles with maple syrup). I ate it all, but slowly, more or less to keep my strength up, mostly. I was definitely at a low point, not just in my search for Cam but maybe in my life so far—not counting our dad's death, of course.

I wasn't ready to totally give up on my virus theory. There must have been something physically wrong with Cam that caused him to collapse on Lisa's doormat. And it was also perfectly possible that Cam *had* dumped Lisa, and she had hated being dumped, and now was sort of getting revenge by...what did they call it—spin doctoring?—the facts in such a way that Cam would look like some kind of a religious/New Age nut.

But there was also a part of me that realized all of the above might be nothing more than a big fat rationalization based on my desire to avoid at all costs facing the fact that my brother was mentally ill.

If you haven't been in the position I was in, you probably have never thought about what it would be like. But anyone who's spent any time walking the streets of any big city knows what "mentally ill" looks like. And the thought of your brother being one of "them" is...overwhelming. Because that'd be like losing him in a particularly horrible way. He'd still be him—the same height, weight, color of eyes, distinguishing scars, and any birthmarks—but he also wouldn't be "him" at all. I counted on Cam, my Cam. How could I stand not having him, *that* Cam, as my brother?

I decided that the best thing for me to do, for the time being, was to avoid, as far as possible, making judgments or reaching conclusions about Cam's condition. I'd try to keep an open mind. Did I actually think I could stop thinking about the cat business and the Aborigine business and the Perfect Being business? No, not really. I guess most of all I didn't want to talk about them.

But as I was finishing my third cup of coffee, I faced a potentially unpleasant reality: I'd soon be talking to my mother. As I just said, I really didn't want to talk about what I'd found out on this little trip of mine, though. So maybe I could keep it simple. My mother already thought that Cam had "problems." Maybe I could simply tell her that his friends, or at least two of them, had noticed that he didn't seem to be "himself" before he'd gone off to the Manor. And then I would tell her that she'd been right (in general) about my trip—that I hadn't been able to pick up my brother's trail as I had hoped I would. That'd please her, in a way.

Beyond that, what I really wished was that I had something else to do right then. Sitting around twiddling my thumbs (even rapidly, after three cups of strong coffee) was the worst. But then I realized the thing I had to do was head straight home for one good reason: in case Michelle called. And *that* made me realize that now—that morning—it had been two days since I'd last spoken to her. It was possible that she'd been trying to get me at my house. I thought I really ought to call her.

The Gramercy Manor phone number was probably right on their official how-to-get-there map, I thought. I paid my breakfast check and went back to my room and looked. And *yes*. It was my turn to say "Bingo!"

I recognized the voice of the woman who answered. It was Ruth the receptionist, the one who'd taken my name in to Dr. Brie, the one who'd seemed a little odd to me.

"Hi, this is Chris Craven again," I said. "I was there a couple of days ago? Asking about my brother Cam?"

"Oh, yes," she said. "You absolutely were. You didn't dream

it, honey. And I got Dr. Brie for you. Would you like to talk with him some more?"

"No," I said. Could she have thought I wasn't sure if I'd been there? Or was she just goofing around? "Thanks anyway. But there *is* somebody else I'd like to talk to, if I might. A Michelle Falk? Could you connect me with her?"

There was a bit of silence at the other end.

"No," Ruth finally said, "I can't. That isn't possible. Michelle's become a member of the dear departed."

"What?" My heart went into a stall and started losing altitude, but fast. "She's *dead?*"

Ruth laughed: a little trill of merriment. "Oh, no, indeed. Or not as far as *I* know, anyway. I meant to say she wasn't here, is all. She's left the campus."

"Oh, I see," I said, now laughing myself. "So would you know when she'll be back?"

"Well, I'm assuming never," Ruth informed me. "I believe she's gone for good. She's outta here."

Now my heart zoomed up the runway and took off. This had to mean she'd heard from Cam; he'd surfaced once again.

"Wow," I said. "Could you tell me where she went, then? How I can get in touch with her?"

"'Fraid not," said Ruth. "I got no information on that subject. It's tough bongos for you, Chris. She didn't leave a forwarding address. Nothing personal, but maybe she just wants to close this chapter of her life. Write 'The End' on it."

"Or it could be she left in a great tearing hurry," I said. "To meet someone, for instance. Do you know what time it was when she took off?"

"I believe it was the afternoon. Nobody knows," she said.

"P'raps you're right. P'raps she went so fast that she was just a blur. No one saw her go, from what I understand."

"Here's something you might know, though," I replied. "Did Michelle get a phone call before she left? Like in the morning or the early afternoon? *You*'d know that, wouldn't you?"

"I *might* know that," Ruth snapped, "because it's my job to answer the phone when it rings. But I can't see where that's any business of yours, necessarily."

"Well," I said, getting a little snippy myself, "suppose I tell you, then. I happen to know Michelle liked my brother, and my brother's disappeared. And now she seems to have disappeared. So I just wondered if—"

"*Everybody* liked your brother," Ruth said, interrupting. It seemed she'd warmed back up to me again. "He was a real cutie pie."

"It's interesting you say that. I'd heard otherwise," I said. "Dr. Brie didn't seem to like him much. He acted like no one did."

"Oh, *I* meant"—Ruth's voice dropped to a whisper, just about—"everybody regular—*you* know."

I wasn't sure just how to take that. I had a friend at school whose mom was an R.N., so I knew that sometimes doctors were a "them" to all the other "us-es" in a hospital: the nurses, therapists and aides, the candy stripers, and the cleaning staff. But if Ruth was a patient at the Manor—even a patient soon to be discharged and working at that desk as therapy—then her "us" would be the other patients, who were just "regular" people, as compared with all those highfalutin mental-health professionals.

But what she'd said seemed like an opening that maybe I could run through.

"Ruth," I said. "There's something that I really need to know and you can tell me. Was Michelle a patient there, or what?"

Once again there was a pause before she answered. I watched the second hand on the electric clock beside the bed go a quarter of the way around the face of it. When she spoke, she didn't raise her voice. In fact, she kept it really low. But she also turned up the intensity.

"Michelle?" she said. "A patient? Why? Did she seem sick to *you?*"

"Well, no," I said. "Or, I don't know. She seemed really nice. But I don't know how anyone can tell...I suppose sometimes you can. But take my brother...."

"Gladly," Ruth responded with a giggle. "And Meesh *is* really, really nice—you're right. And every bit as sane as you or me. Cross my heart and hope to die, big fella."

And then her voice changed still another time, got more authoritative, businesslike.

"No, I'm sorry, sir. This isn't a hotel. We're a private hospital. You may be thinking of the Manor House, in Lennox, I believe it is."

It took me a moment to catch on.

"I think I understand," I said. "Dr. Brie or someone's there. So I'll hang up and hope Michelle will get in touch with me at home."

"Good idea, sir," Ruth replied. If she was a patient, she was a plenty quick one. "Good luck in finding what you're looking for."

And with that we both hung up.

Well, I thought, Michelle is out there somewhere too now. Probably with Cam, but maybe not. So now the question is:

Will she call *me*? Let's say that she'd hooked up with him—would he (who hadn't called me all this time) want her to do that? I didn't know. That was a toughie. It could easily go either way.

But just in case, I thought I'd better head for home, toot sweet. I'd just as soon it wasn't Mom who fielded any call that came from Meesh (I liked it when Ruth called her that) or from my brother. Mom was lacking many of the facts—the *background*—that Inspector C. possessed. *He* wouldn't want some rookie messing up his case just when he got the one big break that sometimes cracks a missing-persons operation wide, wide open. It may seem weird that the possibility of getting a call from an on-the-loose Michelle cheered me up so much, but it did. And that wasn't—I insisted to myself—just a drowning-man-and-straw-type deal.

chapter 10

When I got home, I fed my mom a verbal snack made up of whole-grain truth sprinkled with a few white lies. As per plan, I didn't blurt out any of the...more unpleasant stuff. I definitely was sparing Mom, I told myself. Seeing it was one P.M., she didn't have that bathrobe on.

In other words, I neglected to bring up the cat thing, or the fasting and visions things, or the Proper Living and Proper Being things. So of course I never told her how these things had made *me* feel.

I figured all the true stuff I told her was information she'd probably already gotten from some dean at the University, or from Brie.

"Cam *did* act pretty irresponsibly," said prissy little me, "during his last term at college. Allen York said he didn't care about his course work and was blowing off papers right and left."

I also worked up a glorious technicolored version of Lisa's finding Cammie on her doorstep story.

"I guess he'd been out there for some time," I said. "Lisa said his lips were turning blue and his skin was the color of skim milk. She thought he'd gone into cardiac arrest or maybe had a stroke."

Because I was afraid that when/if Michelle phoned the house she might get my mother—if I was in the bathroom, say—it seemed best to tell Mom who she was. Sort of. And just sort of casually.

"In addition to that Dr. Brie, I had a meeting with a woman named Michelle, who was some kind of associate of Brie's," I said unblinkingly. "She was obviously intrigued by Cam and actually said she'd give us a call if she's ever in this area. I got the feeling Cam was a real favorite of hers."

I chickened out and never did admit my trip was a failure—in that I absolutely hadn't found Cam, as I had confidently assured my mother that I would—nor did my mother remind me of my pre-trip brag. Indeed, she behaved like a good winner and actually apologized for not being more supportive of my desire to go looking for my brother when I first voiced it.

"I suppose I was trying to protect you from the truth," she told me. "Or possibly I was—and maybe still am—in some kind of denial about Cam's…situation. It simply wasn't something I could get myself to talk about."

Well that, of course, was the same way I felt right then, although for slightly different reasons. And so for the next little while we rarely spoke of Cam at all. Neither of us ever raised the possibility of calling the police and making him, officially, a "missing person." I was pretty sure he was too old for milk cartons, but I also wouldn't have liked his picture being electronically transmitted anywhere, or (for instance) thumbtacked onto bulletin boards with "answers to Cam or Cammie" below it. If anyone was going to take my brother into "custody," I still wanted it to be yours truly.

Mom worked for Bronson Realty part-time, which meant

she was out of the house all day on Mondays, Wednesdays, and Fridays. I never went anywhere. Instead of taking the dog for walks, I just let him out in the yard. I didn't tell my mother I was staying near the phone, nor did she ever tell me I should leave the house and look for work or simply get out for a breath of fresh air. It's possible she knew what I was doing; I don't know.

For the first two days that I was home, in addition to jumping up every time the phone rang, I also ate a lot of bacon. Maybe anxiety can cause a person to crave salt, or perhaps I was just ragging on Cam's cat thing and trying to make a pig out of myself. In any case, I had bacon with stacks of griddle cakes for breakfast, and then bacon and peanut butter sandwiches or BLT's for lunch. I also watched all manner of TV, and bathed (as usual) and used deodorant. I might have felt it was important to at least *smell* normal.

chapter 11

On the third day I was home, I was sitting on the living room sofa hooked up to life support in the form of *General Hospital* when the doorbell rang. My mother was out matching someone with her dream house. It was a quarter after three.

I clicked the TV off. Have you ever wanted something so much that you tell yourself it's never going to happen? So: This wouldn't be my brother (I assured myself)—he would have used his key.

And I was right, of course. It wasn't Cam. But it also wasn't the letter carrier, or someone taking a poll, or a pair of Mormon missionaries.

It was Michelle Falk. And looming up behind her another, larger, girl.

"Chris—hi. This is my sister Millie." Michelle sounded no different than she had in the Berkshires, just as friendly and at ease. In our little driveway was a taxicab, which she now waved at.

"Okay," she shouted at the driver. "He's at home." The yellow started backing out.

While that was going on, I snuck a glance at Millie. She was clearly younger than her sister as well as taller—bigger all around with broad shoulders but the same perfect posture: relaxed and balanced, arms hanging at her sides. She wore long shorts, a baggy T, and black leather sandals. Her hair was also black, but cut short just above the shoulders and a little wavy. She was as smoothly tanned as her sister, but her face had bigger features and a more guarded and impassive look. She also looked a lot less glad to see me. She seemed more interested in our front stoop.

"You've heard from Cam," I said to Meesh, just stating that as a fact. "Come in."

"Sure thing," she said. For the first time, I noticed backpacks sitting on the steps behind them.

"Grab our stuff, Mil," said Michelle. "Let's go."

They followed me into the house, into the living room. Millie put down one of the packs and then went straight to the sofa and sat with the other pack on the floor between her knees. She held on to one of its padded straps. Michelle took a quick, appraising look around the room before she perched beside her sister.

"Your mother isn't home?" she asked me, her head cocked to one side as if listening for footsteps—or maternal warning growls.

"No," I said. I checked my watch. "She won't be home for another hour and a half. At least."

"Good," said Meesh. "I'd just as soon you heard this first. It's more to do with you than her, I think. When you've heard my story…then we'll see." She stretched her legs straight out and, leaning forward, touched her ankles with both hands while looking up at me with eyebrows raised. She sure was limber, well stretched out. Darn near catlike, you could say.

I think I shrugged and nodded.

"Here's the story in a nutshell," she said, sitting normally again. "Cam called me at the Manor right after you left. He wanted me to meet him, so I hightailed it out of there—"

"I know," I said. "Without telling anyone. I talked to Ruth."

She looked at me sharply, paused, and said, "So yes. That's right. I didn't think I owed Brie any courtesies."

I didn't care about her and Brie. "You actually went somewhere and met my *brother*?" I said. "You've seen Cam? Just in the last week?" I was trying to chill out, act calm, but there was like a big typhoon inside my head: palm trees, wind-whipped, all bent over.

"Absolutely did. Spent one whole day with him," she said. "He met me at my father's house, a good safe place. But the next day he went down to the store for ice cream and never came back."

She said that in the exact same tone of voice she'd used in our first conversation—in other words, enthusiastically and cheerfully. She didn't sound the least bit angry or upset.

I, on the other hand, could easily have grabbed ahold of her and shaken all her fillings loose. Except that she probably didn't *have* any fillings, going by the brightness of her pearly whites. But—she had had Cam with her and she hadn't managed to *hold on to him*. That really pissed me off.

"He's got her car," said Millie, unexpectedly. "He's had it ever since he jumped the wall." Her voice was a surprise. It wasn't loud, but it was clear and pleasant, almost musical. She'd looked up to tell me that, but then her eyes snapped down again.

"The white Honda's yours?" I said to Meesh. "The one with the New York plates and a Ben and Jerry's bumper sticker?"

She didn't seem surprised that I knew about her car.

"Yep," she said. "I gave him my set of keys before he left the Manor. Then I called up home and told them what I'd done. It was just sitting in my dad's garage. I'd decided not to have anything to do with polluting the air any more, but other people have to make their own decisions. Millie doesn't have a license yet, and my dad, he's got his Cadillac."

"Right," I said to her. "Cam's got your car. *And...?*" I felt unplugged from what was going on. She'd had Cam and she'd let him get away. Indeed, she'd made it possible for him to run anywhere he chose and leave no trail. She could have told me all of this on the phone. She hadn't had to bring her sister and some segment of their wardrobes. What the bloody hell was going on? (Inspector C. was puzzled.)

Michelle was looking at me with those eyebrows up again — as if *I* was the one who ought to be doing the explaining.

But then — at last! — a bit of current sparked inside my brain and lights came on. They weren't planning to stay here.

"Oh," I said. "You think you know where Cam is now, or where he might be going."

Now Meesh looked relieved.

"Yep to the second half of that," she said. "There was this place he talked about. Before, up at the Manor. It's not nearby. It's...far, far away. He found out about it on the Internet, I think."

I don't know why, but I thought she'd almost made that "many moons away" and had switched at the last second. That's probably just me being stupid, though.

"It's a place where everyone believes in simple, basic ways — including self-sufficiency," she said, and smiled. It was such a warm and happy smile I felt myself wanting to confess that those were just the things that *I* believed in — that I was lots like Cam in this way, too.

"The people there are natural and hardy," she went on. "Individualists. Cam corresponded with them — one of them,

65

anyway. He felt a person would be free to fine-tune his senses and develop his own resources out there, free from outside interference."

"Outside interference?" I asked, choosing to stay away from the "fine-tuning of the senses" issue. When had Cam ever been inhibited by outside interference, I wondered—other than during his time in the Berkshires?

"Oh, sure—*you* know," Michelle said with a wave of her hand. "Like at college, where they lay requirements on everyone. Or when people—friends or even members of your family—think you ought to act a certain way, or think like *this*, or just do such and such."

I suppose I nodded just to be polite. In my head, of course, I very much believed that members of Cam's family—and friends—had every right to think he ought to *not* eat cat chow. And it didn't seem unreasonable to me for a college to want people enrolled in it to do…well, college work.

But rather than get axle-deep in quibbles, I sped on to other topics, starting with one of a slightly personal nature.

"Let me ask you this," I said. "When you saw Cam…did he realize *I* was looking for him, that I'd been up where he *was* and all?"

"Yes, indeed. I told him," said Michelle. She beamed at me again. "He definitely was pleased to hear that. 'Good for Chris,' he told me. 'He'll get what's going on. He's sharp. He'll get it.'"

Much as I enjoy a compliment, that one left me more confused than anything. What was this "it" that I was meant to "get"? It looked to me as if Michelle assumed I'd know what he was talking about.

"But knowing I was trying to find him…that didn't make

him feel he maybe should swing by the house to see our mom and me before he took off for...wherever?"

I knew that sounded as if maybe I thought Cam should feel a little guilty if he didn't do that, but hell, I *did* think that.

"No, 'fraid not," said Meesh. It seemed she had no problems with anything my brother thought or did.

"So you didn't come here in hopes of finding Cam in residence?" I asked. I wanted to be sure I had it right.

"No, not at all," she said. "I figure he's long gone from these parts. I'm here because I want to follow Cam, and I assumed you'd want to too. And that you'd consider hookin' up with Mil and me. Three's company, as far as I'm concerned, and we both like good company."

"You *really* think you know where Cam headed for? Where he is now?" I would have liked to be convinced of that somehow—don't ask me how.

She did her best, nodding not just once but lots of times. It was an "absolutely" sort of nod.

"Well, where?" Now, accepting that, I wanted some specifics.

Her face changed. Certainty gave way to doubt, and openness to caginess.

"Don't take this the wrong way, Chris." She used a different tone of voice: the used-car salesman's wheedle. "I like you fine, but I don't *know* you. If I told you where Cam went, you might tell somebody else—your mom, for instance—and she might tell a bunch of other people, right? And then poor Cam might find himself in some bad people's custody and even worse off than he was at ye old Manor. I'd like for you, just you, to get to see him, but never mind a bunch of other people. D'you understand what I'm saying?"

I sort of did, even though I didn't like not being trusted with a secret. As I said before, I don't have many friends. In some ways that gives me a weak self-image, I suppose. But there's a flip side to that, too. At times I see myself as the Lone Ranger, someone you can count on, a guy who sees a lot more than he lets on and can keep things to himself. A righteous sort of dude, in fact, trustworthy as they come.

Of course, I also had to admit (to myself) that if I knew Cam's whereabouts and went gallivanting off after him, I'd probably want to tell my mom where I was going. Just to be considerate—*you* know.

I didn't say any of that to Michelle, however. She had *her* concerns—okay. But I had mine.

So, "Yeah," I said, "I sort of do. But—nothing against *her*"—I looked over at Millie—"I don't understand where your sister fits in. *You* know Cam—you've worked with him and maybe you can help him if he needs your help. He's, like, a friend of yours. But your sister's barely met the guy. How come she's along?"

Before Michelle could answer, Millie jerked her head back up and aimed her huge, intense dark eyes in my direction.

"*Millie*," she announced.

"What?" I said.

"My name is *Millie*," she stated. "I'd appreciate your using my name when you talk to Meesh about me. Instead of just saying 'your sister,' like I was some sort of accessory of hers, like her genuine saddle-leather handbag or something."

Having said that, she looked down again. I wasn't sure, but I thought her lips were twitching as she did so, as if she'd almost had to throw a smile in there.

"Yeah—sure," I said. "Whatever. Sorry." I turned back to her sister. "So how come *Millie* is in the party?"

"Oh, just 'cause she's my buddy," Michelle said. "She didn't like her summer job. She's got another year to do in high school, so at the present time she isn't qualified for anything but scut work. That's all some white men want to give a Mohawk anyway. That or dancing on an I-beam fifty stories up. This was her chance to see the country—some of it—and spend a little high-Q time with me. I was so damn busy at the Manor, I couldn't make it home a lot."

"I see," I said. *Good answer* (I admitted to myself). If I were a kid like Millie—which I guess I am—I'd surely stuff a summer job if I could and then take off and see the country with my older sib. "So—just so I have this straight—the two of you are going to go looking for Cam whether I go with you or not."

"Exactly right," said Meesh. She looked at her watch. "And if it's 'not,' we had better get the lead out." She stood. "You want to hit the bathroom, Mil? I know I'd like to. If you're going to join the party, Mr. Chris, you could pack while we two freshen up."

Millie'd also gotten to her feet by then.

"There's a lavatory in the front hall," I said. "Right under the stairs. I'll go up and get my things together."

You may think that that was awful damn spontaneous of me, to make a big decision all that fast. But I kind of knew that was the only way for me to go: to not even think about it. If I'd started adding up the reasons for going and the reasons for not going, it'd take forever, and I'd end up with two long lists and a big lump of uncertainty in my stomach. Plus, if I waited for my mother to get home, I'd have to factor in her...attitude. I didn't want to deal with that. No, the time had come to let my father's genes kick in again and head out to this haystack of Michelle's.

I went upstairs to my room. Packing wasn't hard; I was in practice. I put the basics in a suitcase, then stuffed in some extra weatherproofing. After that, I sat down at my desk and wrote my mom a note.

Mom:

You remember that Michelle I spoke to you about? The one who worked with Cam along with Dr. Brie? Well, she came by the house and she thinks she knows where Cam is, and she was in a big rush to get going there. So I'm going with her. I don't know how long the trip will take, but I'll give you a progress report every couple of days. Sorry to rush off like this, but I figured it's something you want me to do—for Cam's sake.

Take care—I'll be in touch.
Chris

When I came down, I left that propped against the sugar bowl in the middle of the kitchen table.

Meesh and Millie and their packs were all in the front hall. My suitcase looked sort of formal next to their stuff when we loaded up the car. So I threw in my sleeping bag to show there was a little nature boy in me.

"Which way?" I asked as I pulled out of the driveway.

"West," replied my native guide.

chapter 12

Because I didn't stop to think at all before we left the house, I certainly hadn't thought about what it'd be like to spend some days cooped up in a car with two females. Not that I'd have had anything to compare it to, never having spent more time than a few hours in a car with *anyone*. But now, broadened by experience, I can report that when you're in close quarters with other people over a considerable period of time, you're sure to be (that is to say, become) more conscious of what sex they are. For the most part, this doesn't have much to do with thoughts about having (or not having) sex. It's more a feeling—an awareness—that comes over you. You realize, for a bunch of unrelated reasons, your companions are, on the one hand, unlike you and, on the other, very much the same.

In the case of Michelle and Millie, I first noticed that they had to pee a lot. And "had to" is correct, I'm pretty sure. I doubt they ever asked to stop just to annoy me or to make the trip last longer. My guess is that women's bladders, because they have to share a limited amount of space with other organs guys don't have, are smaller. I don't *know* if that's true, but, hell, it does seem logical.

Michelle maintained that her peeing had mostly to do with how cars affected her. "I don't know if it's the motion or what," she told me early in our second day together. "But put me in a car and I become a *baby*. All I want to do is eat, sleep, and go to the bathroom."

And that was pretty much what she did for the entire trip. She'd claimed the front seat for herself, without discussion, when we first piled into the car. That had been all right with me, because I knew her a little and thought she kind of liked me, while Millie was a total stranger and didn't seem to be much of a talker. But almost at once I learned that my seatmate spent at least a half of every driving day in dreamland. And so over the course of the trip I talked a whole lot more with Millie—about all sorts of things.

On the first afternoon, however, it was mostly Meesh and me chatting back and forth, at first about nuts-and-bolts kinds of things, like cars and highways and how we'd feed ourselves while traveling and where we'd spend the nights. I gathered from this conversation that for reasons of ethnic pride as well as cash-flow problems, the sisters would prefer to sleep in public parks and buy their food in supermarkets. "We're outdoor types," Michelle informed me. "It's mostly men who like motels."

I wasn't wild about their ideas, but because I didn't have un-limited resources myself, didn't know what unexpected expenses might crop up, and (particularly) didn't want to come across as the spoiled, fat, chauvinistic exploiter of the rightful owners of all the land we'd be traversing, I bit my tongue and held it. I also realized I'd probably be able to (a) find a lot of things I'd like to eat in the bakery and deli departments of the average grocery; and (b) treat my passengers to all the luxuries that Tom Bodett could offer, if I whined enough.

Late in that same conversation, Michelle was kind enough

to say that if I ever wanted some relief behind the wheel, she'd be more than happy to take over.

Millie'd spent the previous hour sort of tilted forward, sometimes leaning against the back of her sister's seat, listening to what we were saying but never trying to put her two cents in.

Now, however, she said, "*Uh*-oh!" laughing right away. "You better take out more insurance, Chris. My sister used to be the world's worst driver. And now she's out of practice, even—especially on interstates."

She said that in a kidding tone of voice, and it was all she said, but it seemed to finish off the subject. Meesh didn't argue, nor did she volunteer again. And once I'd seen how easily she fell asleep, I surely wasn't going to be the one to bring it up.

Of course, before too long I had another reason for my silence, too.

It was a little later on the same afternoon that I asked Michelle how Cam had been during the day and a half she'd spent with him at her father's place. She hadn't so much as mentioned my brother's name since we'd left my house, and I'd gotten tired of waiting for her to say something that'd give me an opening I could fill with some of the questions that were fluttering around in my mind about her…whole *relationship* with him. So I asked her how he was when she last saw him. I figured I could then work back from there.

"Oh, he was pretty good," she said. "He'd been trying to put some more of his stuff into writing, and you probably know how that can make him feel."

I actually didn't, because I'd never been aware of Cam doing

73

any extended writing. (In this respect, I resembled his professors at the college during his last term, I guess.)

"I'm sure the Old Testament prophets—some of them—had the same problem," she added. "It's exhausting, the whole process is. Brie and them never understood what he was saying, what he was going through. It was so much more than they could handle, those stupid little rationalists."

"Uh—you're talking about Cam's theories now, like all that 'Perfect Being' stuff?" I asked. It was a little bit embarrassing for me to say—repeat—out loud what Lisa'd said. But that and "Perfect Living" were the two things of Cam's that seemed the closest to biblical to me.

"Sure, but I wouldn't call them 'theories,' exactly," Michelle said.

"What would you call them, then?"

"Well, why not *revelations*?" she said. "Seeing as that's what they are."

I'm sure I shook my head when she said that, and maybe I made a little snorting sound as well. I guess I thought she'd got the word mixed up with some other one—"ruminations," maybe.

"Wait—aren't revelations huge big deals?" I asked delicately. "Ideas that possibly could change the world, or at least the way we understand it?"

"And also like big things—ideas—that come from God?" she said.

"Yeah, right—like that," I answered, still not getting it. "But that wouldn't apply to Cam." I chuckled. "He never even goes to church."

"D'you think those guys in the Old Testament ever went to church?" she asked me.

"Oh, come on," I said. "You're not telling me that Cam was having chats with God, I hope." This was not the sort of thing I wanted to hear from her.

"I'm not telling you anything," she said. Her voice became less cheerful, more defensive. "What you believe is up to you— same as what I believe or what Cam believes. Only two things are for sure: he's a plenty unusual guy, and he's gotten a lot of wonderful ideas from *somewhere*."

I was tempted to pull right off the road and stop the car and face Michelle and tell her I had never heard such bullshit in my life. But instead I kept on driving and tried to make a calm evaluation of my whole...well, *situation*.

I was moved by more than mere politeness. I couldn't help but be aware of Millie breathing quietly a little ways behind my head. She'd been listening to this entire conversation. What could she be thinking? Michelle believed my brother was plugged in to God, apparently. Had Cam *told* her that, I wondered—or might that be her own idea? Either way, it seemed (to me) that Michelle was either very gullible or nuts.

But I wasn't her sister. Millie might have other ideas. Millie might think her older "buddy" Meesh was always right. Millie might be furious at me for not agreeing with her sister. And she was a big girl. Suppose she (just for instance) took her belt and looped it around my neck from behind and pulled with all her might?

And then there was my earlier confusion about Michelle's status at Gramercy Manor. Suppose she'd been a patient, after all? Might sister Millie also be...disturbed?

Finally, that same old same old: Was a perfectly sane Millie, who thought that Cam was crazy, wondering if I was just like him?

I stole a peek at Meesh. Her eyes were closed and she had

75

turned her body slightly to one side and clasped her hands right by her chin. It seemed she'd fallen fast asleep.

There was a sigh behind me and some movement sounds. Millie'd settled back into her seat. Apparently she wasn't going to either kill me or comment on the conversation she'd just overheard. What did that signify, I wondered?

It also occurred to me that I hadn't commented about it to her, either. I wondered if she wondered what *that* meant.

In fact, my silence might have had something to do with my not being sure what kind of comment *to* make—if, let's say, Michelle was right, and my brother did think he was being spoken to by God.

My feelings were also made more complicated by this: To the extent that I'd had any religious education that really "took," it had come from Cam.

Maybe I'm not being completely fair to my Sunday school teachers when I say that, though. They certainly did introduce me to a lot of biblical facts, like the slinky goings-on in the Garden of Eden, and one of them had gotten me to be a little Calvin Klein with crayons, when I colored Joseph's coat. I'd also learned about the Wise Men from them, and what "hallowed be thy name" actually means, and the grisly details of Jesus' death, and a lot of other age-old information.

But it was Cam who had convinced me—I must have been about twelve at the time—that God was this cool gender-less presence who wanted me to be myself and to enjoy myself but also to try to avoid hurting anybody (including myself). Cam had made God...well, you could say *personal* for me. "A lot of people think they're big," he told me, "and that they have all the answers and can do anything they want to anyone. You've probably run into some teachers like that. And some kids, too." I'd nodded my 100 percent agreement with that, and he'd smiled and nodded, too.

"But they're all full of it," he went on. "They can have the *power* over you, but that doesn't make them right, or better. We're guys or women, and we're all in the same boat. As soon as you start thinking you're better than somebody else, little brother, you're on the way to becoming a real big jerk."

A lot of times Cam would tell me these things soon after I'd gone to bed. He'd come into my room and sit in a chair near the head of my bed. I'd loved the little talks we had at night. One night he told me it was okay to pray for stuff but not to expect that what I wanted and what God wanted could necessarily be the exact same thing. "I do think God likes hearing from us, though," he'd said.

It may seem odd or surprising that Cam, at sixteen, was into believing in and telling me these sorts of things, and more. (He assured me, for instance, that no one's religion was any better than anyone else's, and that "lots of scientists" believed that the complexity of the human body itself proved the existence of God.) But this was Cam, don't forget, the guy of many interests and enthusiasms—which he'd often share with me.

If he'd always believed God talked directly to guys like him or me, I know I would have heard about it at some point. So what he'd said to Meesh—and Lisa—was definitely something new.

chapter 13

The next morning we ate our first supermarket breakfast in the car. Mine was a quart container of orange juice and most of a box of thickly sugar-frosted cinnamon-raisin bakery rolls (I saved one for a mid-morning snack). All that went on top of two cups of the bitter free coffee that the market brewed each morning for its customers. Millie and Michelle (who'd made no reference to our God conversation the day before) ate crunchy handfuls of cornflakes out of a huge box they bought, and washed them down with swallows of milk. Millie was obviously the experienced shopper; she had an envelope of coupons with her, and she whipped one out that, doubled by the store, allowed her to get a dollar fifty off the corn flakes. She also checked all the milk prices carefully before deciding that the gallon plastic container of the store's own brand was too good a value to pass up, even though we lacked refrigeration in the car.

"It'll still be fine at lunch and dinner, too," she assured me (having waked up talkative, apparently). "And there'll probably be enough to sell *you* a few swigs if you want some. Seeing you're our driver, we'll be offering you a real good deal."

As I groped for a polite way to turn down her offer (inasmuch as I was neither a big milk drinker nor prepared to do saliva swapping with this pair), she grinned and added, *"Kidding!"*

Then, when they'd finished their hand-to-mouth meal and

closed up the cereal box, the resourceful Millie dug several small bottles out of her pack and extracted pills from same.

"Our vitamins," she said to me after she'd popped a couple into her mouth, slurped milk, and swallowed. It really seemed as if she wasn't holding yesterday—my argument with Meesh—against me.

"Cam believes—and I do, too," said Meesh, "that if you produce all your own food—organically, of course—and thereby know exactly what you're taking in, there's no real need for extra vitamins. But eating like we're doing now, it's best to pop some supplements."

I was tempted to ask her what kinds of vitamins you'd need to supplement a diet of canned tuna fish and cat chow, but I decided not to. If she believed that God endorsed those kinds of meals, I didn't want to hear about it.

One thing I thought I noticed, though, was that Michelle (perhaps unwittingly) seemed to pop a little more than Millie did. I wasn't sure, of course. There were a lot of bottles and a lot of passing back and forth of gelcaps, pills, and that big jug of milk. Because I wasn't offered any of the pills, I wasn't sure which vitamins were being downed, or what their potencies were. It was possible, I realized, that one of them was helping Meesh to fall asleep. I'd read somewhere that some vitamins are particularly good at counteracting stress. I don't know. Maybe Meesh believed she needed bottled relaxation to offset the excitement of a quest that had my brother subbing for the Holy Grail.

That day, we stopped in Harrisburg, Pennsylvania, so that Meesh and Millie could take each other's pictures outside the state capitol. Michelle believed that people wouldn't believe them if they said they'd visited so-and-so-many states on their trip. I mentioned that going to a lot of capitals might mean we wouldn't be taking the most direct route to wherever we were going, but that didn't seem to matter to Meesh.

She laughed and told me if we had to zigzag some, that'd be fine. "It'll throw them off the track," she said.

I laughed along with her, assuming that it was just a little joke of hers, pretending we were fugitives or something.

When Michelle fell asleep after lunch (a peanut butter and strawberry jam extravaganza)—she'd already napped briefly after Harrisburg—I wondered if Millie'd follow suit. And because she wasn't sitting directly behind me, I had to fiddle with the rearview mirror to find out.

I guess my doing that caught her attention, because when I got the mirror aimed at her, she was looking into it and smiling in what seemed to me to be a friendly way. She definitely had a light-the-room-up smile.

"No, I'm not asleep," she said. "I want to see this big ol' country when I have a chance to."

"Me too," I said—softly so as not to wake up her sister. I was happy she'd spoken, actually—glad to have a little (conscious) company. It can get lonely in a car.

"So I guess I'll skip the nap, myself," I said. That was a pretty lame joke, but I saw her smile at it anyway—as if to give me credit for the effort, maybe. She was acting differently than she had inside my house, for sure: less formal, more *inviting*. I thought, she's actually really pretty.

"You don't have to whisper," she told me. "Meesh could sleep through a metal concert—swear to God. I wish I could help with the driving, though. I know how, but only on an automatic. My father lets me chauffeur him around sometimes. When he's been drinking, mostly. His car's a Cadillac, an '82, a great big thing. I've never had it on the highway, just around the neighborhood." She talked fast in that pleasant voice she had, as if she was in some big rush to tell me stuff.

"Haven't you had driver's ed at school?" I asked. "That's how I learned to drive a stick. My mom has an automatic, too."

"I *should've* had it," Millie said, "but my father wouldn't let me. He said he didn't like the man who taught it. He said he'd heard the teacher took advantage of young Mohawk girls"—she laughed—"when he got them in a car behind the wheel. So my dad told the school it was against our religion to drive."

"It's against the *Mohawk* religion to drive?" I asked. That didn't seem possible; Mohawks have to get around, like everyone else.

"No, no," she said, and giggled. "All the other Mohawk kids took driver's ed. No, he said it was against our *family's* religion, that we'd hooked up with some particular sect since Meesh had been in school. I forget what he said it was called."

"But they must have known *he* drove," I said. "That he had his big long Cadillac."

"Yeah," she said. "But he told my school he wasn't a very good whatever-it-was, but he was bringing *me* up strict."

"He sounds like a character, your father," I said.

"That's what people say he is." She might have sighed. "The ones who like him, his good buddies. My mother didn't think so, though. She bailed out when I was six. I think she'd had it with

81

my father's...lifestyle." She laughed at that, but not as if she found it all that funny.

I was curious, of course.

"I guess he's a guy who wants things a certain way," I said, trying to be diplomatic *and* fish for more information.

"You can say *that* again," she said, now sounding—I don't know—resigned.

We were in eastern Ohio at that point in the trip, heading for a campground near a town called Senecaville. Michelle had chosen it as a good place to stop because the Senecas were the westernmost of the five tribes that made up the Iroquois Confederacy, the Mohawks being the easternmost.

In any case, this part of Ohio is dotted with lakes and ponds of all shapes and sizes, and that might have had something to do with the presence of a turtle in the road ahead of us.

Automatically I pulled off onto the shoulder and stopped.

"What's up?" asked Millie. She hadn't seen the thing, I guessed. She seemed concerned about us stopping out in the middle of nowhere.

"Stupid turtle on the road," I said. And I unbuckled my seat belt and climbed out of the car.

It turned out to be a full-size painted turtle, quite a handsome fellow. He retracted head, legs, and tail (why do I think of all turtles as being male?) as soon as I picked him up, and I carried him in the direction he'd been heading (toward the far side of the road) and put him down well off of it, in the trees and near a nice wet ditch. It looked to me like just the sort of place a traveling turtle would check in to. A Reptile Inn, ATA approved.

When I got back into the car, I snagged a paper towel off the roll I keep under the driver's seat and wiped my hands. Millie was leaning forward and regarding me with what appeared to be (at the very least) *intensity*.

"What did you do—kill it?" she asked me. Her voice had changed again. She could have been about to cry.

"*Kill* it?" I said. What did she think I was? "Of course not. I just put it near a ditch over there—a perfect place for it. I didn't want it to get run over."

"Oh," she said. "I thought you sounded mad. At it, I mean. When you said 'stupid turtle' like that." It seemed that she'd relaxed a bit.

"I wasn't *mad* at it," I said. "I don't even really think it's stupid. For all I know its turtle IQ's a lot higher than mine. It isn't its fault it doesn't know about eighteen-wheelers. I wouldn't either if I'd spent my whole life in a mud hole."

Girls can be funny about animals, I thought. But I still wasn't prepared for her next question.

"So—is it sort of like you think of turtles as your *brothers?*"

I reached down for another paper towel, and yes, I certainly was stalling. Did she believe that turtles were our brothers? Relationships with different species could be very different in her culture. For the moment I'd forgotten that she'd spent some time with Cam.

"Not exactly," I said slowly, busy buckling my seat belt and then starting up the car again. "I just think that they're a part of nature, and that they shouldn't be killed by, well, *machines*. Unnecessarily. What do you think?"

"I think...about the same." Now she sounded...I don't know, confused. "I just wasn't sure what *you* might think." I heard her flop back in her seat.

"I'm sorry, Chris," she said after a moment, softly. "I ask too many stupid questions...."

Maybe it was the way she said that, as if it wasn't all she would have liked to say. Or maybe I just got one of those glimmers of understanding that probably everybody gets from time to time.

"You've been waiting for me to say or do something crazy, haven't you?" I asked her. "Seeing as I *am* Cam's brother."

"No, really—I . . . Well, yes, maybe I have," she said. "Oh, I don't know. Your brother seemed so sweet. But he definitely has some strange ideas."

"You can say that again," I said, echoing her remark about her father. I think I hoped to make a sort of bond with her by saying that, by repeating something she'd said.

"Families," she said.

To that I nodded solemnly, not ready yet to risk some other guesses.

Michelle, as if that single word had summoned her from sleep, groaned and stretched.

"Well, look who's up in time to see the sunset," Millie said. Now lightly, jokingly.

Subject changed. Amen to that, I thought.

We didn't stay at the campground near Senecaville after all. As we passed one of its parking lots, Michelle saw a man going into a trailer.

"It's Dr. Brie!" I heard her say—and in a terrified tone of voice.

"What? Where?" I said. I hadn't noticed anyone.

"Back there," she said, pointing, still very agitated. "Going into a trailer. I swear."

"Come on," said Mr. Reasonable, "it couldn't be. First of all, I don't think he's the trailer *type*. And what are the chances that out of all the places in the world he might be right now, he'd end up in the same obscure campground in Ohio that we were planning to stay at?"

"Well, maybe it wasn't him," Meesh said. Millie had a hand on her shoulder and she seemed to have calmed down a little. "But it *could've* been. He might be looking for Cam. He hates it when a client walks away. And I'd just as soon he didn't know I'm...in the picture." Before, back at the place, she hadn't seemed afraid of Dr. Brie at all, but clearly that had changed.

I moved the mirror so's to take another peek at Millie, but she didn't look at me this time.

So rather than argue with Michelle, I headed out of there. She'd only just woken up, so maybe she was still half-dreaming, in that never-never land between sleep and wakefulness. That was one explanation, anyway.

The other one, of course, was the one that had danced in and out of my mind ever since I'd first set eyes on her at Gramercy Manor: that she'd been a patient there, too, that she was at least a little screwy. Ruth, the receptionist, had semi-denied it, but not really, and now I was seeing for myself. Her belief that Cam had gotten information straight from God had made me have real doubts about her ability to...distinguish between the real and the unreal. But her "seeing" Brie was even worse. That seemed like a genuine hallucination with paranoid overtones. There was no way a Dr. Brie would chase two former clients across the country. That would only happen in an oddball movie, or in a dream, or in the mind of someone who had been (and still should be?) a mental patient. Yikes.

chapter 14

The next day we visited two state capitals, Columbus, Ohio, and Indianapolis, Indiana, and doing that slowed us up a lot. It wasn't that either one of them was off the beaten track; a major highway ran to and through them both. No, what took a lot of time was getting off old Interstate 70 and finding the capitol building, and then parking, walking over to it, taking the pictures, etc., etc., etc.

A person who was less afraid of rocking boats than I would probably have asked my passengers at some point in the day if the purpose of this trip was finding a brother or comparing traffic densities in major midwestern cities (while fantasizing about being shadowed by a jerk psychiatrist). But Craven, Chris, did not. I may have groaned a lot and even muttered curses at the traffic, but for the most part I repressed.

The fact that it was hotter than hell made everything just that much more annoying and unpleasant. So by the time I called my mother, shortly after we'd located an acceptable campground not far from the Illinois state line, I wasn't in the best of moods.

Nor did it seem as if my call was going to make my mother's day.

"Chris!" she shouted out by way of greeting. "I can't believe you.... Where on earth are you?"

"Illinois," I said evasively. "And in the middle of a monstro heat wave. You can't believe how hot it is out here. People keel right over in the street—it's what they call the fried-brain syndrome. Even the money in my wallet's soaked! And there's no relief in sight, they say."

It wasn't that I was looking for sympathy particularly. It was more that the weather was the safest subject I could think of. Not that we stayed on it for long.

"Uh-huh," my mother said. "I just about flipped when I read your note," she added. Sometimes she tries to talk the way she thinks I talk. It's another of her bathrobe things. She may know that it annoys me.

"I couldn't believe it!" she went on. "Who is this Michelle person exactly? Is she a doctor? How old is she?"

A lot of that was my mother's way of asking if Michelle was good looking. She seems to live in constant fear that some gorgeous babe is going to "wrap me around her little finger." Hey, I wish.

"I don't know," I answered. It was time to mix and match: a little truth, some falsehood. "Old enough. Not, like, a kid. I don't think she's a medical doctor. She's some sort of therapist, I guess. She spent a lot of time with Cam up there. She was the person he confided in."

"So she says he told her where he was going to go when he...escaped?" my mother wanted to know. "Why didn't she just stop him?"

"It wasn't like that," I told her, making it all up as I went along, of course. "It was more Cam saying the kind of place he hoped to live in some day. You know the way people talk. It's like you saying you want to move to Aruba."

"Yes, but I'm perfectly aware that isn't going to happen," said my mother. "This is different. How do you know you aren't on a stupid wild-goose chase?"

"I don't know that!" I snapped. And the reason I snapped was probably that I'd been thinking the exact same thing myself all day. "But it's like before. I didn't have a lot of choices, and it was driving me crazy sitting around the house doing nothing."

"Well, you could have gotten a job," my mother said, reasonably enough. "Reasonably," in my experience, is apt to suck.

I heaved one of my real super-sighs, the kind that says *"Mother!"* without saying it.

"So where exactly are you headed for?" she asked.

I'd already figured she'd ask me that, and I'd decided it was much easier to make up an answer than to try to change the subject. And you never know, maybe what you make up can turn out to be the truth.

"Eastern Montana," I said promptly. "Some big ranch out there. It belongs to the family of a guy Cam knew in college. I think their name is something like Whitman—or McLain, maybe. Some name like that. The guy used to go on and on about how great it was out there, and I guess Cam decided it sounded perfect for a person like him. You know how crazy he is about the great outdoors." Sometimes I'm amazed by how believable my lies sound.

"Well, to me a ranch in Montana sounds like a jumping-off place," my mother said. "But you're right. *He* might like that." She paused. "And this Michelle seems to think she can find it?"

"She's got directions," I said. "I haven't seen them yet, because we're nowhere near the place. But she got directions to it somehow."

"Suppose—and I think this is really unlikely—but just suppose you *do* find Cam. Does this woman think she'll be able to persuade him to come home?" my mother asked. By calling Michelle "this woman" my mother was letting me know she couldn't stand her. Most people I dated soon became nameless: "that girl you're spending so much time with."

"Or might she get him to go back to Gramercy Manor?" she continued. "Suppose he doesn't want to go home *or* go there? What then? Has she thought of that?"

My mother's no dummy. She didn't expect answers to all those questions. She was just beating me up for taking off the way I did.

I let her hear that sigh again.

"*Mom,*" I added to it this time. "Let's us just find Cammie first and then worry about all that. What I plan to do, when and if we get to where he is, is just stick with him." I know I was making up policy as I went along, but what the hell. It *sounded* sensible. "As long as I'm with him, I can make sure he's safe—that's number one—and that he doesn't do anything that'd get him into trouble. And all the time what I'll be trying to do, of course, is talk him into coming home. And Michelle will be doing the exact same thing."

I guess there wasn't anything my mother could object to in that plan.

"All right," she said, only a little grudgingly. "Seeing as you're halfway there already, probably, you might as well keep going. But call me the *second* you get to wherever this ranch is, all right? That shouldn't take more than a couple of days, should it? Is the car behaving all right? You have your Visa card, I hope."

"Yeah, yeah, yeah," I said. I realized what my mother had accomplished in that last speech of hers. She'd given me permission to do what I had, in fact, already done: go off and look for Cam. Then, after that, she'd asked some typical mother-type questions, maybe trying to reinstate or underline our traditional roles: she being the mother/superior and me the son/subordinate. Although I didn't like my part, I sure was used to it, and I did still want to please her, make her proud of me.

"I'll call in a couple of days, regardless," I now told her. "Everything's fine. Don't worry, Mom. I've got a good feeling about this trip. Cam probably just needed to get away for a while. I'm going to find him at this ranch, and before you know it we'll be back together—all three of us."

After that, there wasn't much for either of us to say. For the time being, I was out of her control—if still not fully independent—and I think we both knew it. Maybe that scared us both a little. Was this to be the start of something, such as my adulthood?

Well, be that as it may. I was glad my mother'd never met Michelle and that she didn't know there was a second person (female) on this trip.

chapter 15

I got to know that second person, Millie, somewhat better on our second night out of Springfield, Illinois, which was the next state capital after Indianapolis. We spent it not that far from Sioux Falls, South Dakota.

The heat wave we'd been trapped in didn't let up all that day, and in late afternoon huge thunderheads began to gather straight ahead of us. My idea of heaven at that point was simple: an air-conditioned room, a long cool shower, clean white towels (they didn't even have to be fluffy), and a bed I could collapse, spread-eagled, on. (Oh, and unquestionably a lot of tasty, filling food.) None of the above are campground staples, of course, so I started talking up motels.

My point, made as we drove along, was that we ought to get one really good night's sleep before we hooked up with my brother, and inasmuch as up ahead it looked like either a torrential downpour or the end of the world, tonight might be the perfect time to put ourselves in the hands of the *Mobil Travel Guide*, my treat.

Millie turned out to be quite friendly to that plan (Meesh appeared to be asleep, as usual), and so with the day rapidly darkening, the wind picking up, and lightning flashing straight ahead, I pulled into the driveway of the Lampost Motel.

"Triple-A approved but getting an F for spelling," I said, chuckling. Michelle stirred in the seat beside me.

When nobody agreed or disagreed with what I'd said, I added, "Lamppost has two *p*'s in it." Was I showing off? Of course.

"Are you sure?" said Millie. "One p *looks* okay."

"No way," said Mr. Smarty. "Lamppost's like 'withhold' or 'roommate.' Double letter in the middle. It just *looks* a little funny."

"*You* look a little funny, but that doesn't mean you're right," said Millie unexpectedly. I quickly checked the mirror. She was grinning. "I used to win a lot of spelling bees in grade school."

"But you're out of the little red schoolhouse now," I told her, almost biting my tongue over that "red." I mean, all I'd meant was…*you* know. "This is the big time, baby, and you're up against a pro." I leered into the mirror, hoping to take her mind off of what I'd said before—I mean, if it had been there at all.

"The only spelling pro that I believe is Mr. Webster," she informed me with another grin—thank God. "And until he shows me otherwise, lamppost has one *p*."

"Okay," I said. "And if you're so crazy about ones, you'll probably also insist I just get *one* room for the three of us tonight." I said that in a slightly pissed-off tone of voice. "So, fine, I guess—that'll save me a few bucks, anyway. You and Meesh can share one bed, and I'll make do with the other one. I just hope neither of you snores." Then I crossed my fingers mentally, actually hoping that she would call my bluff. I'd never come close to spending a night with one girl, let alone two, and the thought of doing so was, frankly, pretty scary. Not that I'd never fantasized…that kind of stuff.

Millie made a rude noise with her lips, and I relaxed. "No way we're sleeping in a room with *you*," she said. "I'm not risking my sister's and my reputation by shacking up with an alleged misspeller. It's either separate rooms or take us to the nearest campground, buddy."

I made a show of being shocked at her uncool but actually gave in to her demand quite quickly. So she shook Michelle awake and told her what the deal was.

Sleeping Beauty took one look out the window at the weather we were in for, yawned, and told us, "Super-fine with me."

The shower and the towels were average, but the dinner that I had in the Lampost's dining room was an American classic, just about. The girls both had it, too, and I helped them finish theirs.

What we ordered was the evening's Blue Plate Special: Yankee pot roast with mashed potatoes and green peas, and pie à la mode after. The plates were thick and king-size and actually *blue*, with that willow design on them. The portions were enormous. And the food was *good*, especially the gravy and the pie. I told the waitress that I hoped I'd marry someone who could make a meal as good as the one I'd just had.

"Me too," said Meesh.

The waitress looked at her. "Well, Harold—he's our chef— ain't married at the moment, but he's kinda partial to them blondes with the big bazongas, if you know what I'm saying."

"Shucks," said Michelle, sounding disappointed.

"I know," the waitress said to her, and sympathetically. She was stick slender, older than my mother. "But Harold's also sixty-two and's got a rug. You'd be better off with someone closer to your age."

We couldn't tell if she was serious or kidding.

chapter 16

I was stretched out on one of the two beds in my room by eight thirty, pretending I was Lewis on the first night back from my expedition with Clark. At ten I turned off the TV, and within minutes I was fast asleep.

When I woke up, the digital clock in the radio beside my bed said 11:48. For a second I thought I'd overslept and was at home, where there's also a radio with a digital clock in it beside my bed. Then when I realized it was still dark outside and that I wasn't home, I wondered how come I was awake at such an hour. As a rule, my sleep is steady, undisturbed.

An explanation came at once: There was a gentle tapping at my door, maybe seven or eight taps. Someone was insistent; someone wanted me. I turned on the bedside lamp and got out of bed.

"Yes?" I said cautiously, my mouth a few inches from the beige metal surface of the door. I had on black and green plaid boxer shorts, and nothing else.

"Chris—you awake? It's Mil," I heard her say.

I forgave her the ridiculous question—who did she think said "Yes?" The waitress? I'd put that little chain thing on the door, so now I coughed to cover up the sound of my undoing it. Then I cracked the door about six inches.

"Yeah—what?" I kept most of me behind the door but stretched my neck so I could see out of the opening I'd made. She had on the same baggy shorts she'd worn the first day that I'd met her, and a mostly black T-shirt that I'd never seen before. It said STOP HYDRO-QUEBEC on it in white letters in the middle of an octagonal red stop sign.

"I thought I ought to tell you..." she began, but it didn't sound as if she really wanted to. She was looking at my carpeting. And she seemed to have come to a dead stop in the middle of that sentence.

"Tell me what?" I prompted her. Then, because it seemed so rude to leave her standing speechless on this outside covered landing, "Do you want to come in?"

I opened the door wider. I wasn't used to entertaining girls when I was wearing only undershorts. She came right into the room. I noticed she was barefoot, too. Her feet were sizable, but also...shapely. Not big fat clodhoppers like they could have been.

"We had a little accident," she said slowly. "Not just now, earlier. With the phone cord."

I'd shut the door but still had my hand on the knob; she'd stopped about three steps past the doorway and had turned in my direction, but she continued to check out the floor. When she started talking again, she spoke much faster and darted glances up at my face every few words.

"I tripped over the darn thing, clumsy me," she said, "and it pulled right out of the wall. This isn't one of those jack things. It's the whole wire. We'll pay for the damage. I don't want you getting stuck with that, and it wouldn't be right to just take off and not say anything. It could be a little bit expensive. They may have to run a whole new wire in."

95

When she finished, she looked up at me a final time with a little forced smile on her face. Her dark eyes seemed shiny in the half-lit room.

"This is something Meesh did, isn't it?" I said. I don't know how; I just knew. "You can tell me how it happened. I'm sure she didn't do it just for fun."

I wanted very much to touch her as I said that—make some contact, other than with words. But then I hesitated, standing there, awkward in my boxer shorts. She went and sat on the end of the extra bed, head down again.

"No," she told the carpet, "she didn't do it just for fun. She thought the phone was bugged—or I don't know if bugged's the right word, or what. After she'd pulled the wire out of the wall, she told me Brie'd put a microphone in the receiver, some listening device, so he could hear every word we said." She shook her head. "She's sleeping now. I gave her something."

I joined her on the end of the bed. Our hips touched when I sat down.

"She was a patient, wasn't she?" I said. "The same as Cam. Not the *same*, of course"—I corrected myself—"I mean, everybody's different. But up there because she had some problems."

Millie started nodding, and I could see a silvery tear tracking its way down her smooth cheek.

"Yes," she said. And suddenly she lifted her head and turned toward me, and this time she didn't look down again.

"She can be *fine*," she said—as if daring me to contradict her. "When her medication's right, she's perfect. You'd never think she had the least thing wrong with her. She doesn't, really, actually. It's just a chemical imbalance that she's got. I'm trying to adjust her medication now. She's helping me. That's how well

96

she really is—that she can do that. We should have started days ago. She'll probably be better...like, *tomorrow*."

After she said that, she still didn't look away, and there were more tears rolling down her cheeks. I felt like someone in a play who knows he's meant to say something. At that moment, though, the only lines that I could think of were real weaklings, platitudes like "I'm sure she will be" or "Let's hope so." Lines that didn't sound the least bit wise or helpful.

So instead of saying anything, I grabbed her by both upper arms and kissed her.

She didn't seem to mind. She didn't slap my face or leap up to her feet (with an oath) or even pull her head away—oh, no. Instead, to my amazement and delight, she kissed me back, and in a way I wasn't that familiar with. Maybe "hungrily" describes it. But whatever the word, there's no getting around the fact that she really put herself into that kiss. It really seemed as if she wanted it and maybe even on some level, *me*. None of the earlier kisses I'd received in my life had seemed to have that quality.

This was a real Ferrari of a kiss, compared to all the Tonka toys that had preceded it.

After a time, a little while—I've no idea how long—she pulled her head away from me. Our hands were still on one another—she wasn't, so far as I could tell, rejecting me—but our lips were suddenly a foot or so apart. Mine were slightly open; I believe I was panting.

"I'm being a big baby," she announced in an emphatic whisper. "This isn't fair. I'm taking advantage of you."

In a different situation I'd have laughed, given her the old hee-haw. But this was not a moment for the old hee-haw. This wasn't light and easy. She'd just admitted that her sister was a nut case.

So, naturally, I simply told her, "No, you're not." I didn't feel taken advantage of at all, and I didn't see anything babyish about her crying when she really had something to cry about. And God knows there'd been nothing babyish about that kiss; God would *certainly* know that.

"If you're anything like me," I said to her, "what you are is slightly overwhelmed by... well, this whole situation. For one thing, by not knowing what to do a lot of the time, or even what to think. *You* know—about everything." I knew I was babbling, but it was 100 percent all-wool honest babble; nothing going on was clear or definite.

"There've been times I've thought this whole trip was a bad idea," I said. "I mean, the looking-for-Cam part of it. Sometimes I get really sick of thinking about him and trying to figure out what's the best thing I can do for him. But every time I have those thoughts I end up feeling guilty about being a lousy brother, and I tell myself I ought to be a whole lot more tuned in to what he's going through right now. Or, trouble is, I really can't imagine what it's *like* to have the thoughts and... well, the *feelings* that he's having."

Millie nodded this time and brushed her hair back from her face. I thought she looked beautiful, like maybe a young Hawaiian queen. I was pretty sure the Mohawks didn't have queens, so I couldn't say that, but she definitely looked different and a whole lot more... *exotic* (I guess the word is) than the girls I go to high school with.

"How can anybody know what's best for someone else?" she said. "I can't even figure out what's best for me a lot of times. Or what's 'right,' or 'kind.' What's the kindest thing I can do for Meesh? How the hell do I know?"

"At this point," I said, "I can't imagine not keeping on going. If we *could* find Cam, that'd be something, I don't know what, exactly, but something. And maybe if we found him, it'd become obvious what our next move ought to be." I gave a little shrug.

"Right," she said. She got up off the bed. "And short of locking her up, there's no way anyone could stop Michelle from going looking for him. I'm pretty sure she loves the guy—no matter how she is, *you* know. Or at least she thinks she does. Or whatever."

She started for the door.

"Look," I said, "I'll take care of that phone business when we check out tomorrow. Leave it to me, okay? And one other thing…"

"What?" She turned back toward me.

I didn't say anything; I just stepped up and grabbed her. That was such an un-me thing to do, I could hardly believe I was doing it. But I loved the fact that I was doing it as well. I loved not being me.

We kissed a second time.

This one was more of a big Lincoln Town Car than a Ferrari, probably, but it was also good. She didn't pull away. There was no mention made of "fairness" or "advantage" afterward.

But yes, I might have had this (somewhat un-me) thought: "Oh, baby!"

chapter 17

After Millie left my room, I got back into bed but didn't turn out the light right away. Darkness is for sleeping, and there was some thinking that I had to do.

For one thing, I had to think about those kisses. Possible mistakes? I'd initiated both of them, which made me, in a way, *responsible*. I mean, when someone (such as Craven, C.) kisses someone else, initiates the kissing, I feel he's sending her a message in which words like "like" and "need" and "want" comingle. He doesn't have to spell it out, and she doesn't have to be able to spell "cat" (let alone "lamppost") to understand it. And in this case her return kiss had fairly shouted "like" and "need" and "want" right back at him.

Was all of that okay with me? I had to ask myself. Had I, caught up in feeling sorry for a teary girl, *lied* to her by kissing her? Would I have liked and needed and wanted her if, say, we'd met in English class or at a party?

Well, I wasn't totally sure about that, but the point was we hadn't met that way, and our relationship was based in part on the fact that I had a brother and she had a sister who some people had said were mentally ill. And that gave us something in common that was considerably more major than a shared fondness (or distaste) for the poetry of Robert Frost or the flavor of Bud Light. Furthermore, for the foreseeable future it was going to be up to the two of us, acting in concert, to make decisions that would certainly affect our loved ones' lives. We *needed* to feel close to each other.

But—I told myself—even without that particular need being part of the total picture, it was fair to say that Millie was a lot of ways I like a girl to be. She was laid-back rather than bubbly or loud. She had a good sense of humor, in addition to intelligence. She didn't look like everybody else, and the way she *did* look was a turn-on. She kissed great.

I smiled, lying there with my hands clasped behind my head. Those kisses *hadn't* been a mistake. "Good move, Chris," I told myself. It looked very much to me as if I had my first real girlfriend. And how, pray tell, did that feel? Fabulous! She'd not only help me find my brother but would also figure out what I should do for/with him.

That made me bring Cam front and center. And also made me remember the sadness on Millie's face when she was telling me about Michelle and the telephone wire. And *that* got me to thinking again about how awful it must be for Cam to be this other "person" who everybody—except Michelle and that Ruth, the receptionist at Gramercy Manor—considered to be out of it, at least to some degree, a certain amount of the time.

I realized that in all the hustle and bustle of *doing* stuff— going here and there and dealing with a lot of different personalities—I'd sort of lost touch with my brother, with his situation, and with how much a part of me he was, how much he was embedded in my heart.

For all my life, up until very recently, Cam had been "amazing" in a good way. I'd always idolized him. Without him, I don't know how I'd have coped with our dad's death or with not being a regular average guy. Cam made it clear the way I was was *much* better than "average," no matter what the wiseguys in my homeroom said. Growing up, I'd borrowed confidence from his seemingly inexhaustible supply of the stuff. If Cam—whom everyone looked up to and believed— could say that I was "wonderful" and "special," how could I doubt that? He was the rock I'd built my self-esteem on.

I guess you could say he was the *architect* of it as well, in some important respects. You know how when you're growing up and there's all this stuff you kind of wished you knew more about, or all about, and you feel really stupid for not knowing, but you're embarrassed to ask anyone about, especially your mother? And other stuff you don't even realize is important, but it is? Cam said all this material, which should be common knowledge, was only known half-assedly by lots of kids, and he asked me did I want to learn it.

"Sure," I said. "I guess."

"Good," he said. "Let's shake on that." He held out his hand, and so of course I had to take ahold of it.

Cam cupped his other hand behind his ear while that was going on. "Interesting," he said. "Your handshake's saying something loud and clear."

"What's that?" I asked, going along with the joke.

"'I'm a loser,'" he informed me. "It's saying 'I'm a big fat wimpy loser.' But it doesn't have to, Chris."

And before I knew it I was practicing "the right way to shake hands": chin up, looking the other person in the eye, grasping the whole hand, not just the fingers, firmly but not painfully. It was actually sort of fun.

"It's nice to see you, Christopher," said my instructor about the sixth time that we shook.

"My pleasure, Mr. Cameron," I replied.

"Now." He rubbed his hands together. "Let's move along to an important automotive matter: How to Give Someone a Jump Start."

After that came...let me see...The Right Way to Fill Out a Bank Check (I made out practice ones, for enormous sums, to the order of "Dunkin' Donuts" and "Neiman Marcus"), followed by How to Deal with Almost Anything That Goes Wrong with Your Toilet, and then A Woman's Body and How It Works. That last one took some time. Together we read the book *Our Bodies, Ourselves*, which, Cam said, made up somewhat for the fact that neither one of us actually *was* a woman.

Remembering all that kicked off a massive mood swing: I started crying. Cam had done so much for me, but now, with him maybe being the needy one, I couldn't see what gifts I had to bring to him, what "common knowledge."

And now that I knew the truth about Michelle and the shape that *she* was in, I had to wonder if she really knew thing one about my brother's present whereabouts.

I turned over and put my face in the pillow. What was going to happen next? Suppose Cam *wasn't* where Meesh took us? And even if he *was* there, how would he like having us show up? What if he refused to even talk to us? Cam had never taught me How to Deal with Mental Illness in Your Family.

103

I'd told my mother I had a "good feeling" about my finding Cam when I first started looking. I surely had a different feeling now.

Millie was great fun to kiss, but what did she have to offer in the way of answers to all the questions I had? I reached out and doused the bedside lamp without looking at it.

It was absurd to be so big and feel so absolutely helpless. Talk about being babyish: All I could think about was that I needed Cam, my Cam, *right then*. Facedown, I pressed the pillow up against my ears and sobbed, wrapped in that one thought, until I guess I drifted off to sleep.

chapter 18

In the morning things looked better, as they often do. Black moods grow fast in darkness but shrink down or even disappear in morning light. What I was left with was a kind of hangover—a dull ache, the residue of the sadness and self-pity I'd indulged in. I felt a bit ashamed and very glad that Millie hadn't seen me carrying on like that.

Before I'd finished with my shower, I had made a plan. I'd talk to someone in the motel office and arrange to have the wiring in Michelle and Millie's room looked at while the three of us were at breakfast. Then when I paid our bill, I could settle up for everything. I'd make up some ridiculous story about one of them wanting to unplug her hair dryer and mistaking the phone cord for *its* cord and giving it the mother of all yanks.

As I was toweling off, I allowed myself some thoughts concerning Cam. It now seemed I'd been a lot too negative the night before. I didn't know for a fact that my old Cam was gone for good—not at all. It was important for me to remember that for about 99 percent of his twenty-one years Cam had been just fine. Sometime in the last few months a tiny part of his circuitry had shorted out or otherwise been changed or damaged. But who was to say it couldn't be repaired? Almost every month, it seemed, you'd see a story in the paper or in a magazine about some doctor learning something new about the human brain, how different stimuli—chemical, social, or environmental—could make it misbehave. I reminded myself as I put on my clothes that even during the periods of time when Cam was saying or doing some pretty far-out things, he wasn't doing them *constantly*. It wasn't that all sorts of people at his college had gone to the dean or medical director to report this raving lunatic in their midst. Also, Dr. Brie had admitted to me that because of his bad attitude my brother hadn't been *treated* at the Manor, chemically or otherwise. Cam could get better as quickly as he'd gotten worse, I told myself. It *was* common knowledge that most people who had "nervous breakdowns" managed to make full recoveries, wasn't it?

We had a hearty breakfast in the motel dining room, or at least Millie and I did: melon, platters of eggs and sausages, stacks of toast with jam. Having a girlfriend hadn't dulled my appetite, it seemed. The food was served by a different waitress from the one we'd had the night before. This one could have been in high school still. She told us that her name was Pegge, with two *e*'s. Though Meesh didn't join us in the full-course meal, she did have a large grapefruit juice and most of a Danish and coffee—and she seemed completely fine to me. Apparently the changes in her meds that she and Millie had worked out were doing the trick. At no point did she claim that Dr. Brie had managed to transform himself into the Seeing Eye dog (a handsome yellow Lab) who'd stretched out on the floor beside a fellow diner's chair.

It was sort of…interesting…seeing Millie for the first time

since our relationship had...matured (or deepened, or—to put it mildly—gotten so much more exciting). Typically, she didn't dodge the issue by acting nonchalant or coy. No, when the three of us joined forces in the dining room, she looked me right in the eye with a little special smile on her lips. I'm pretty sure Meesh didn't see that smile. It would have been a giveaway. I felt a little rush of pride to be the one that she was smiling at. I'd never caught that kind of smile before.

We collected another state capital that day: Pierre, South Dakota. To do so, we had to leave the major east-west highway we'd been on and go due north for thirty-some miles through this huge stretch of prairie. After the official photos had been taken and we were all back in the car, I automatically turned around and headed south again. It was then that Michelle grabbed the road atlas for the first time and started studying it. Up until that point she'd plotted our course by telling me which capital to head for next; the choice of routes she'd left completely up to me.

"We're heading back to Interstate 90 now?" she asked.

"Yep," I said, "that's right."

"Okay. So when you get there, hook a ralph," she told me.

"Hook a *what?*"

"A ralph—a *right*," she said. "Aincha got no culcha?" She was grinning.

"Okay, got it," I agreed. "You want us headin' west on ol' nine-o. But just in case you fall asleep again..."

"Right." She took the hint. "What I figure is, we'll camp near Rapid City somewhere." She was looking at the map again. "Maybe a little past it. Seems like there's a place not far from Spearfish—what a great name for a town, don't you think?

There's one called Deadwood, too. Look here, Mil. You see where I mean?" She passed the map back to her sister.

"And then tomorrow…?" I was staying cool; my tone of voice was 100 percent casual.

"I'll tell you how to go when we get rollin'," Michelle said. "We make an early start and possibly we'll sit down to lunch with Cammie-boy. But now"—she yawned—"I do believe it's nap time."

We followed her directions: found the not-too-far-from-Spearfish campground, shopped for some supplies, sacked out. I decided not to ask Meesh any questions and just wait for morning, load the car, and let her take us to…wherever. In the course of doing all the things we did that day, I managed to make eye contact with Millie a number of times and even *touch* her, just offhandedly, when it was possible to do so. We never were alone, so I didn't have a chance to kiss her, but I was pretty sure she knew I wanted to. There's a kind of telepathy between people like the two of us, I think. I, for instance, was very sure *she* wanted to, right back.

When we got going, we didn't head for an interstate. In the course of the morning, in fact, the roads we traveled on became increasingly secondary; I imagined them getting thinner and thinner on the map Meesh was staring at, and going from red to blue. Traffic also thinned; it seemed most vehicles out here were pickups. When we came upon a gas station sort of out in the middle of nowhere, I stopped and got a fill-up.

Just before noon we arrived at a small town (I'm not naming it on purpose), and Michelle said, "This is where we ask for more directions, someplace."

I parked and let her take her choice of places. A post office, luncheonette, tavern, garage, and a superette were the only possibilities, two on one side of the street and three on the other. She chose the post office. It looked as if our destination wasn't in Montana after all.

While she was inside, I turned around and said to Millie, "Here we go, I guess."

She grabbed the seat back and leaned forward to kiss me on the lips, just a quick peck for good luck was how I thought of it, but it made me feel—don't laugh—more confident. As if I could handle...*it*—whatever happened next.

When Michelle came back to the car, she was smiling, and she had a little piece of paper in her hand.

"It's about fifteen miles," she told me. "The guy said we can't miss it."

By the time we were two miles out of town, we weren't seeing houses anymore. There were occasional private roads or driveways, some of them pretty rutted, but you could never see where they led to: sometimes the land was cleared and sometimes it was woods. Meesh had me take a left and then two rights. The roads we traveled on were narrow blacktops with no lines on them.

I glanced at the odometer. "Fourteen miles to here," I told Michelle.

"It should be pretty soon, then—on the right," she said. And a little farther on, "Look—there! That's it! Turn in!"

"It" was another dirt road heading into some woods. The sign at the head of it read SOL2, neatly printed in black paint on a rough-sawed board.

We turned in. The road had grass in the middle, but the

car's bottom didn't scrape; telephone poles were running along-side it. After about a quarter of a mile we came out of the woods and into an open space. It didn't look like cropland, as if any-thing had ever been planted there; it was just that whatever grass and weeds and brush had been growing there had recently been trimmed down to about a six-inch height, or less. About a hundred yards ahead of us was a barbed-wire fence with a gate in it, and beyond the gate the ground rose sharply and the road continued up with the utility poles still bringing civilization right along with it. At the top of the rise I could see a couple of buildings made of logs, which were partly hidden by some trees.

The gate was all wood and had big metal hinges. The fence on either side of it consisted of five strands of taut barbed wire attached to sturdy wooden posts. The lowest strand was less than a foot off the ground, and the highest one seemed only a little lower than the Honda's roof. In the middle of the gate was another sign. This one said:

> DO NOT PROCEED BEYOND THIS POINT
> WITHOUT SPECIFIC PERMISSION
> FROM THE MANAGEMENT

I'd stopped the car a few feet from the gate, and now I opened my door and got out. I didn't have any plan in mind when I did that; it was just something to do instead of sitting in the car. I was wearing a gray T-shirt and jeans and a baseball cap that Cam had gotten for me up in Burlington, Vermont, at the Magic Hat brewery. I'm not a great one for hats, but this was about the coolest baseball cap I'd ever seen, and I'd stuck it on that day for luck. So I felt okay about my appearance, in case anyone from up at the house was looking down at me through binoculars. I also wanted them to see I didn't have a gun. It just popped into my mind that people might like to know who was armed and who wasn't out here in the Wild, Wild West.

A moment later the girls got out too, both of them in sleeveless tops and shorts. Clearly they, too, came in peace.

"I don't see anyone," I said to them.

"Maybe they're having lunch," said Millie.

"Let's honk the horn," suggested Meesh.

So I got back in the car and honked. Three times, in fact. Then I got out again.

It didn't take long for the honks to be answered. Someone had a bullhorn up there. His voice had that electronically amplified sound you hear on cop shows on TV.

"Whatever it is you want, we aren't interested," it said. "In other words, skedaddle. Oh—and have a nice day."

I looked back at our car and shrugged.

"Tell them who you are," suggested Meesh. "And why you're here."

I cupped my hands around my mouth.

"I'm Chris Craven," I shouted. "Cam's younger brother. I understand he's here. I drove out to see him."

There was a long enough pause to make me wonder if my voice had carried up there. Or if this guy was deciding whether to shoot me for not "skedaddling" right away, as I'd been told to do. For some reason I just assumed the person with the bullhorn also owned a big high-powered rifle.

"You drove here from *New Jersey*?" the same voice asked, sounding (I thought) both incredulous and contemptuous.

"Right!" I hollered back. "I'm pretty sick of driving."

There was a brief silence, broken by a new voice saying, "And I suppose your friends are sick of driving, too. Who the hell are *they?*"

"They're sisters," I replied. "Michelle and Millie Falk. Michelle is a friend of my brother's."

"I see," he said. "Wait there a minute." This person sounded like someone in authority, like a boss, or a vice principal. In fact, this *was* a little bit like high school, I thought, where people you couldn't see spoke into microphones and gave you orders. We stood there like three obedient little freshmen, waiting.

"Okay, Chris," he said, once he was good and ready, "you back up your car a little ways and get it off the road. You won't have to lock it. Then the three of you can enter by the gate and walk on up here." We started to obey. "Close the gate behind you. That's the spirit."

Being told that made me pretty—actually, *completely*—sure that Cam was there. And, in fact, that knowledge also made my heart beat much, much faster.

Weeks and weeks before, when I'd first decided I was going to go and find my brother, I'd known that there was one sort of chancy thing about the whole enterprise. Even if nothing whatsoever was the matter with Cam, it was quite possible that he'd be completely (and irrationally) furious if I found him.

For Cam did have a temper. I don't fly into rages, but he does. I'd known that all my life. Everyone knew that: his friends, his teachers, our mutual mother, for sure.

It wasn't that he was "bad-tempered" in the usual sense of the word. Cam wasn't even what you'd call a moody individual.

No, as a rule he didn't mind being kidded or interrupted or argued with. And as I've said, he devoted hours of his time to me up until he left for college, never making me feel like a burden or a pest. In fact, if you asked me to put down my brother's temperament in writing, I'd probably use words like "easygoing" and "humorous." And then, reluctantly, I'd add an asterisk.

That was because he did from time to time—maybe a couple of times a year—get really, really angry.

Except "get really, really angry" doesn't do justice to Cam's furies. "Explode" is more like it. "Lose it" works. "Go bananas" sounds a little too lighthearted, although you might use those words after the fact, when he'd calmed down and gotten back to normal and was apologizing for the mess he'd made or the damage he'd done.

It was impossible to predict when Cam would blow—what incident or event would set him off. It might be something that anyone would be apt to get upset about, like when he was told he ought to mind his own business by a teacher after he'd written a letter to the school newspaper accusing the administration of looking the other way when gay students were being verbally and even physically abused by members of the football team. Or it could be something trivial and ridiculous, like the time the pizza place screwed up our order and sent one over with anchovies on it, which he despised.

Cam's anger never took the form of violence against another person, though. He never assaulted the pizza delivery guy or anyone else. But he did attack *stuff*: that pizza, walls, doors, dresser drawers, a big glass jar he'd almost filled with spare change. And he did…well, *scream* is definitely the word, though he would probably prefer "roar."

113

These rages lasted just a few minutes and if he was at home almost always took place in his own room—he'd run to it and slam the door before he cut loose. The one that happened at school…I guess it was lucky he calmed down on his own before someone called the cops and asked them to bring over a dart gun or a straitjacket.

So I had some cause for apprehension as I went to meet my brother. I remembered Michelle had told me Cam knew I was looking for him and that he'd said "Good for Chris. He'll get what's going on." But that wasn't the same as him saying "Tell Chris I'll be at such-and-such a place, and he should come and join me pronto." The truth was, I *didn't* get what was going on at all, and it was quite possible that my stupidity (or whatever it was) would set my brother off.

All that was on my mind as I was starting up the hill.

chapter 19

We were on the road, about halfway up the hill, when Cam appeared from out of the trees near the summit and started walking down toward us.

First reaction (mine): Relief; he *is* here—*great!* Second reaction: Wow, he sure looks different. Third reaction (took the form of a question): Should I be *running* up toward him? Do I dare?

Deciding not, I waved enthusiastically instead, and started walking faster. Those seemed to be good moves. He waved right back, but he didn't start running either, and neither did Michelle. I could see Cam smiling broadly, as if he was really glad to see me. Big relief.

The closer he got, the more he looked familiar, although maybe older—thinner, too. What was most different about him was his hair. Now it was much longer, shoulder-length, lighter, and tied back in a ponytail, curly-wavy still. And his hairline had receded farther, on both sides of center, and he was very tan. You couldn't miss the tan; all he had on was a pair of olive-green shorts held up by a wide black belt. Attached to the belt and snug up against his right hip was a big bone-handled knife in a brown leather sheath.

As he got closer still, I noticed that his feet were covered by a pair of dusty soft-soled moccasins and that he had a rawhide thong around his neck from which hung a small silver cross and what appeared to be the tip of some animal's horn with several holes drilled in it. There were wide silver rings on two of his fingers and another piece of rawhide around one wrist.

His eyes seemed very bright and his teeth very white, perhaps because his skin was now so tan.

"*Frater!* Chris!" he said when we were only steps apart, and he spread his arms out wide.

Of course I hugged him—was delighted to. His skin was warm and dry and his hair smelled just a bit of wood smoke. I was conscious of my own wet armpits.

When we broke apart, he hugged Meesh too, and then Millie.

"What a super-size surprise!" he said when that was over with. "All three of you out here! But how on earth…?" He looked at each of us and with both hands pointed first at his gut and then at all the real estate around us. How did we ever find him? he was wondering.

"You mentioned this place," said Meesh. "And that you'd written back and forth with someone here. Remember? At the Manor? We'd been talking about heaven."

I was pretty sure Cam didn't recall that conversation, but he covered up real fast. "Oh, sure—yeah, yeah—of course," he boomed, a huge smile on his face. "And you remembered—all this time."

He was reaching back and turning on the charm full blast; Meesh gave a little wiggle of delight.

Then, serious, he said to me, "How's Mom? I'm such a *louse*.

I should have called you two, or written. I've been...well, awfully *occupied*, but hell, that's no excuse. Just tell me that she's...dealing with everything all right."

"Well, yes, I guess she has," I said. "She's been worried, of course—not knowing how you were or anything, but overall..."

"Good!" He cut me off; he clearly didn't want to dwell on Mom's morale. "I know you'll set her mind at ease when you get home." He turned to Meesh then. "These are good people here—receptive to a lot of my ideas. We mesh extremely well in many ways."

Then he looked down, stroking his chin, as if he was trying to remember something or figure something out.

"But what exactly are you *doing* here?" he said to me—or possibly to all of us—when he looked up.

"Well, basically I wanted to see you," I said. "Maybe have a chance to spend some time with you. Meesh and Millie hooked a ride with me. Meesh was the guide—she thought she could find this place. And Millie came along to keep us company." I wanted to be sure he understood that the three of us were not Siamese triplets, that we all had different roles and different agendas.

"Right, right," Cam said. "But as far as you spending any time here goes, that may not work—be possible. I'm just a guest myself, you realize. I don't get to say who stays or goes."

"I saw the sign—the one out by the road?" I said. "SOL2? Are those someone's initials? Like, the owner's? Solomon Oswald Lonesome the Second?" I said that with a nervous giggle.

"No, actually, the owner's name is Arthur Honeycutt," said Cam. "I'm going to take you up to meet him in a minute. SOL2 stands for Sons of Liberty Two. The second coming of the origi-

117

nal Sons of Liberty, in a way. You probably learned about the first Sons in school—Sam Adams, Paul Revere, those guys?"

"Sure," I said. "There were lots of different little groups of them, weren't there? Sort of like secret societies?"

Cam nodded. "Same deal here," he said. "The movement's in its infancy, just taking shape. I think it's got some real potential. There may be a place for me in this."

"How excellent!" said Meesh. "It's absolutely beautiful out here. So different from back home, so spacious. If freedom had a flavor, bet you'd taste it in this air."

I looked past her at Millie at the end of that. She didn't look at me.

"Well, let's go up," said Cam, "so you can meet the guys." He clapped me on the back. "There are men up here the likes of which you've never met before. Wonderfully instinctual beings. They can feel, for instance, *rightness* in their bones. It's not a thing they've had to study, learn about."

We continued up the hill to the compound, with Cam serving as our tour guide. Now I could see clearly the two big structures made of logs. Cam called the two-storied one the main house and the other one the bunkhouse. The latter, he said," was empty now, but it could fill up on weekends if there was "something doing."

"Art Honeycutt, Sandy, Fred, and Jesse all live in the main house," said Cam. "And so do I if I'm not out roaming around somewhere."

The other sizable buildings were the shop and the barn and the warehouse—all with unpainted rough-sawed boards for siding. The springhouse and the shed were smaller tar paper structures.

Michelle looked all around and said, "My God! This looks so *perfect!*"

The bottom floor of the main house was mostly one huge room with knotty-pine walls and a beamed ceiling and four big posts down the middle for support.

At one end of it was the kitchen, which featured all the stuff you'd find in a regular kitchen, only king-size, with the big items being dull metal or stainless steel (instead of white enamel), more like what you'd see in a diner than what's in your home. Near the cookstove was one of those circular chandelier-type deals with hooks that had all kinds of pots and skillets hanging off them, and the knife box on the counter must have held a dozen blades.

The opposite end of the room was furnished like a living room, with sofas and lamps and side tables and upholstered chairs, a glass-doored gun cabinet, and a big cast-iron woodstove. Between the kitchen and this sitting room were three long picnic-type tables with benches along both sides and captain's chairs on the ends of them. And it was at one of these tables that four guys were sitting.

When we came in, they stopped talking and all turned their heads to look at us. None of them stood up.

"Well," said Cam to them in this really jolly tone of voice that also seemed to be a little deeper than his usual, "here we have my brother, Chris, and his two lovely sidekicks, Michelle and Millie."

Then to us, "Guys, I'm pleased to introduce our host and owner of this spread, Art Honeycutt..."

He was the one in the chair at the end of the table: fiftyish, with neatly trimmed, short reddish-gray hair, and a gray sea captain's beard (no mustache), a weathered face with a long pointed nose and light eyes, either blue or green. He nodded, looking at each of us in turn. Ever been "sized up"? That's how I felt then.

"And on his right, Sandy Prime..."

This one smiled and raised a forefinger by way of greeting. He looked to be late twenties—early thirties and had on a camouflage jacket with the arms chopped off, no shirt, and a tan as good as Cam's. His hair was very straight and blond and tied back in a loose ponytail; his eyes were blue and wide, and he wore an amused expression on his face. He was the type the girls in my high school called drop-dead cute.

"The sizable presence across from Sandy is Jesse Brink..."

"Sizable" was right, all right. Jesse Brink looked to be even bigger than me, a beefy man in his middle forties with a considerable gut on him. He had a fleshy nose and a red face, and I thought he had the kind of looks that the cook at my mother's grandfather's lumberjack camp would have had. You could imagine him heaving sacks of flour into a wagon. The coffee mug he held looked small in his big hands.

"How ya doin'?" he said to us agreeably enough.

"And beside Mr. Brink, Fred Slocum," my brother concluded.

Slocum was leaning forward with his elbows on the table. He, too, was middle-aged, and he had on a soiled blue baseball cap with a gold S on it that was set on his head a little off center and not pulled down low, the way we wear them back home. I thought he looked like a farmer, but one who'd known hard times and maybe missed some meals. He told us "Hiya" with a little jerk of his head, and when he did I saw that he could have

120

used some dental work—quite a lot of it, in fact. He seemed more shy than hostile, though. He and Jesse both wore long-sleeved work shirts—green and blue, respectively—neither of them clean and crisp like Art's, which looked more military with those little straps on its shoulders.

I felt that I should say something.

"Very pleased to meet you," I got out. "Thanks for letting us come up. Like I said before, we've been on the road a long time, and it's nice to get out and stretch."

When nobody said anything back, I added, "It sure looks beautiful around here. And wild. You can't get privacy like this back East." I shook my head and forced a chuckle as I said that last part. I was trying to fit in, I suppose, and say the sort of things I thought these guys would like to hear.

"I guess you can't," said Arthur Honeycutt. "And it's a goddamn shame, the way I look at it." His was definitely the boss's voice I'd heard through that bullhorn.

He pushed back his chair and stood up. "We just finished eatin'," he went on, "but there's plenty left still, as you can see. So you just set and help yourselves. I'll get you plates and Cam can heat the coffee up."

I don't know if his getting up was a signal or not, but the other three rose too, picked up their plates and mugs, and took them over to the big metal sink, which had a pile of dirty dishes in it already. That Brink *was* a man mountain, towering over Sandy Prime and even over Slocum, who was a six-footer himself, but skinny. Prime was one of those guys who does everything—even clearing a table—with a kind of lazy grace. I was sure he'd be able to climb a tree like a monkey, punch the stuffing out of almost anyone, and dance a mean lambada.

121

"You guys gonna pick that load up now?" said Honeycutt, and all three nodded, heading for the door.

Prime was the only one to speak. "Later," he said, touching one finger to his forehead and then flicking it in our direction with a little smile.

Watching him—and the two others—leave the room, I couldn't help wondering what Cam was doing with this bunch of guys, how he could think he meshed extremely well with them.

Cam's friends had never looked much like these four. They'd always been a lot like him—in other words, smart, curious, his same age, if not rich certainly not poor, "educated," and suburban. I believe Jerry Kloss, his best buddy in high school, was Jewish and Brian Martin was certainly African-American, but it didn't mean that Cam sought out "diversity" in his relationships at all. I don't think he was what you'd call an elitist either, but the various interests that sort of took him over didn't leave him much time or energy to put into trying to forge friendships with people who were different. That was even true when he was scouring the Internet for civil rights stuff. On the face of it, I would have said that he had nothing in common with Sandy, Jesse, Fred, or Art Honeycutt. In his previous life he probably wouldn't have had anything to do with those four. Not because he was a snob, I insist (again), but because there wasn't anything I could see that they could base a friendship on.

Another thing that had surprised me a little was Cam's looks, the appearance thing. It wasn't that he looked bad or unhealthy, it was just that he seemed to have adopted a...style that he'd always sort of put down in the past.

I guess what I'm talking about wasn't all that extreme, just a lot of little things that added up. The long hair in a ponytail, the stuff around his neck and the rings, the big Tarzan of the Apes knife. Cam had always dressed conservatively; he was boxer shorts and not bikini underwear—no earrings and not even tempted to tattoo. While the old Cam probably would have also carried a knife in country like this, it would have been a clasp knife he kept in his pocket.

"Chris," he'd said to me more than once, "there are a hundred better ways to call attention to yourself than looking like a freak. And if you don't believe me, ask ninety percent of the good-looking girls you know."

No, I thought, although it certainly was my older brother that we'd found, this seemed to be a...how shall I put it?... different *version* of the guy. A Cam who didn't seem quite right to me.

chapter 20

"There's plenty left still," Arthur Honeycutt had said, speaking of the food on the table, and in a way, I could see why. Not that anything was *wrong* with their lunch. I'd eaten everything laid out there, and worse, a lot of times. It's probably that in my imagination I had guys like these eating dishes out of *The Chuck Wagon Cookbook*: barbecued wild boar on biscuits, or a fragrant, meaty buffalo stew.

But what the girls and I sat down to was a half-empty Tupperware container of cold baked beans, sliced bologna, and sliced American cheese (both curling slightly at the edges and still in their torn-open wrappers), part of a loaf of supermarket white bread, and mayonnaise. Also on the table was a half-gallon container of milk, a number-five can of fruit salad with its lid off, a sugar bowl, and a ravaged bag of Oreos.

Art brought us clean plates and mugs and spoons, and then, instead of returning to the captain's chair, he went and perched on a stool by the window nearest the front door. There he was close enough to chat with us while also keeping an eye out for the mail or the UPS truck or whoever he expected to come knocking on the gate below.

So when Cam got to the table with the blue enamelware

124

coffeepot—steam now rising from its spout—he assumed Art's place at its head. Michelle, Millie, and I had already gotten into being benchwarmers.

I wasn't that surprised when Meesh began to rave about the food in front of us.

"God, I just about grew up on baked bean sandwiches," she told us as she started to construct one. "Except we didn't have bologna with." She laid a slice of bologna on the beans, smeared mayo on a second piece of bread, and slapped that down on top. "This is *definitely* my kind of lunch."

She bit into her sandwich. A dollop of the bean filling squeezed out and dribbled from the corner of her mouth onto the front of her top. I thought she looked like a cute but slightly bratty little kid—except that you could see her nipples up against that sleeveless top.

"That right?" said Art, sounding interested. "Whereabouts did you grow up?"

I made my own bean and bologna sandwich ("when in Rome...") and listened to Michelle expound on the Iroquois Confederacy and what territory it had once controlled and how little of it she and her fellow tribespeople could now call their own—including the New York town that she'd been born and raised in.

"Your people's great-great-granddaddies made one basic, elementary mistake," said Honeycutt. "They trusted the authorities, the government of the United States. The Founding Fathers had some great ideas, but their successors down in Washington"—he shook his head—"turned out to be one bunch of power-hungry sonsabitches after another."

"This is about the best coffee I've had since we left my house," I threw into the ensuing silence, raising my cup to our

125

host. "And the sandwich is great, too. I've never eaten one of these before."

"He's the one from New Jersey," Millie said teasingly. "God knows what kind of weirdo food they eat down there—besides saltwater taffy."

"I'm not sure I ever talked with someone from New Jersey before ol' Cam called up," said Art. "About the only easterners we get out here besides the tourists are federal agents. Cam's more like someone from this county here. He's got his head on straight."

"I've been showing Art that easterners are not all bad," said Cam. "There's lots that we two have in common, starting with the things we feel about responsibility and self-sufficiency. And man's relationship with God and nature."

Uh-oh, I thought; here comes my brother's Perfect Living rap. But no. Our host apparently had chewed on that already.

"Your brother here," said Arthur Honeycutt to me, "is one smart so-and-so. I don't know about him getting stuff direct from God, though. Hell, it's in the Bible that God gave man dominion over the spotted owl, and the goddamn coyotes, and the grass on the prairies, and the lumber in the forest, and the gold and silver in the ground. Anyone that can read knows that. But your brother's learned a bunch of other things, too, somehow. Not in any goddamn college, either. Including how to take off into the woods, dressed like he is right now, and with nothing in his hands or on his back, and come back days later looking like he'd been out for a five-minute stroll. There's guys who've lived here all their lives who couldn't do that, I promise you."

"Cam's been making believers out of people ever since high school," I said. "He's always had a following."

It seemed to me my strategy should be agreement: with Cam, with Honeycutt, with anything that anyone with any power or importance thought or said. To me, Cam clearly wasn't "right." But Honeycutt wouldn't see that, necessarily. He might think Cam was a little bit eccentric, but basically he seemed to admire him. The biggest problem facing me, I thought, was how I'd ever talk my brother off this "spread" and get him back to someplace where he could be helped. Clearly he was happy here and had managed to fit in—so far. But in the long term...well, I couldn't imagine going off and leaving him in a place like this.

"So," said Arthur Honeycutt, "I'm supposing you three'd like to spend the night with us. There isn't a hotel or a motel real close at hand. You girls could bed down in the bunkhouse, and Chris could have the extra bed in Cam's room. Were you thinking you'd keep on going to the coast—seein' as you've got this far? I believe that's what a lot of tourists do."

He didn't seem to be speaking to any of us in particular, so Millie, Meesh, and I all looked at one another, maybe hoping someone else would answer.

"It's Chris's car..." said Meesh, but when she didn't add to that, I thought I'd better throw my two cents in.

"We don't want to be in anybody's way," I said, "and we sure appreciate your being so hospitable to unexpected guests. We'd really like to spend the night, if that's okay. What I was hoping was I'd be able to spend a few *days* with Cam before we push on. We could maybe—like tomorrow—check out the nearest motel and take rooms there for a couple of nights, and Cam could drive out and meet us in town for part of every day. And then...and then he could maybe tour us around the area a little, show us some of the sights and different points of interest."

127

I could see Millie nodding supportively out of the corner of my eye. I wasn't sure how Cam and Meesh were taking what I'd said.

"Well," said Arthur Honeycutt, "along those lines, I was thinking Cam should take you on a hike this afternoon. You two brothers could start to get caught up, and he could show you some of the country he's been exploring; you can't get lost if *he*'s with you. And like you said, I'm sure you all could stand to stretch your legs after all the setting you've been doing."

"Now as far as tomorrow's concerned—" Meesh began, but Honeycutt cut her off.

"Honey, let's not bother with tomorrow yet," he said. "The boys are picking up a load of stuff—a shipment we've been waiting for—right now, and depending what-all's in it, we may be making different plans the next few days. We'll know better later what our schedule's going to look like."

"A hike sounds great to me," said easygoing Millie. "I was starting to go nuts cooped up in the car. I mean, we zipped right by so many places I'd have liked to go exploring in. I bet there's some great wildlife around here. I bet everything's bigger than what we've got back East."

That got Art Honeycutt off and running, telling us about not only elk but also about all the other wildlife that he'd offed in his career, both here and in the Rockies. Hunting story followed hunting story while the three of us munched Oreos and with our spoons chased pieces of syrupy pear and peach and pineapple—and even the odd grape—across the surface of the plates we'd used for sandwiches before.

When it seemed that he'd wound down, and we had drained our coffee cups a final time, Michelle made a point of getting

Millie over to the sink, where they got busy on the dishes stacked up there.

Mr. Honeycutt just sat there on his stool and kept on peering out the window. Uncertain what to do, I took a step in the direction of the girls, but Cam grabbed hold of my arm and shook his head.

"That's all right," he told me softly. He didn't have to spell it out; I got the message. We were in a place where men brought home the bacon, and the ladies got to cope with all the greasy pans.

chapter 21

Our hike? Exceptional, to say the least. Unusual. Revealing.

Begin with what I learned about my brother's outdoor skills. I mean, I'd known he was interested in all that stuff and had some experience. But I'd never really seen him in action before.

The thing is, when I was growing up, Cam and I *talked* much more than we did stuff together. I guess that'd be the way it is with most brothers who are four years apart in age. I often wasn't "ready" to be deeply involved in the kinds of things Cam got interested in. For part of the time, in fact, I was so busy adjusting to the activity of my hormones and the size I was becoming, it was hard for me to get interested in anything else. I did a lot of sitting around, but that was fine in a way, because whenever Cam felt like talking to me about anything or informing me about some part of life I ought to know about or think about, I'd be sitting around in my room or the family room (where our TV was), and he could find me easily. And I'm sure he enjoyed sitting around with me some of the time. It never occurred to me that he'd assigned himself the role of father substitute or anything like that. No, it just seemed as if he *liked* me. Which, of course, has a good deal to do with why I was so crazy about him. Other guys my age seemed to be constantly fighting with their older brothers. I seldom even had an argument with Cam.

But anyway, back to our hike and the things he talked about. Animal tracks, for instance. They told him lots beside what animal had made the track. Listening to him go on, I was reminded of those Sherlock Holmes stories in which the great detective is able to deduce what kind of underwear a guy has on by looking at his mustache.

"Here we have one nervous deer," he said at one point, crouching beside some marks I hadn't even noticed when I passed them.

"He's a heavy, full-grown buck," Cam went on. "His big barrel chest makes his toes turn out a bit—you see? Right here he's stopped. He's listening, twisting his head right and left, checking sounds from all directions. See the way these prints are? He's rocked on his feet a little, same as you would if you turned this way and that.

"His big ears really help him listen. Looky here." Cam cupped his own ears with both hands. "I can hear four times as far this way. Try it."

A little later he had us checking out animal droppings as he explained all the info they provided about the animal's health and what its taste in fast food was. Though he didn't show us any of *his* droppings, he explained that a tracker's diet had a great effect on his tracking skills. I think he said you shouldn't eat a lot of grease or birthday cake, but that nuts and berries were okay. As he went, he nibbled on various wild edibles he found along the way; there was this one seed he said a person could live on for days—just a lot of them, eaten plain and raw, with some water. I could imagine someone wanting to track down a bunch of pork chops and some mashed potatoes while eating a diet like that. And while he was on the subject of tracking, he showed us the quietest way of walking when you're trying to sneak up on an animal: a kind of slo-mo goose step.

And one more thing—oh, yes—he gave us a quick survey of the region's geological history.

This was, I thought, my brother at his best. He'd collected a lot of information from all sorts of different sources, and he could share his knowledge in a way that turned his hearers on. As I've said before, the guy's a great enthusiast. It was easy to get caught up in all the stuff he had to say as we meandered through this lovely countryside.

After about an hour and a half of mostly steady walking, Cam suggested stopping for a rest. I imagine he was just being considerate of his big load of a brother and the girls; he could clearly keep on going all day long, nonstop.

Of course he chose a neat-o spot for our break, in the shade of some tall evergreens and beside a pretty little brook. And it was there that I brought up the Sons of Liberty Two.

"Oh, well, I guess they are a little paranoid," said Cam in answer to my question about the fence and the sign and our first greeting on arrival. "But it's in a stand-up-for-the-little-guy sort of way."

"How do you mean?" I asked. I'd taken off my shoes and socks and was dipping my size thirteens into the cool running water.

"The roots of their beliefs, their attitudes, are in their 'issues,'" Cam explained.

And with that he went into an extended rap about a guy named Randy Weaver out in Ruby Ridge, Idaho, and his family. I'd seen a TV show about that whole mess, how this Randy, a religious fundamentalist with a Nazi-like belief in white supremacy, had holed up on a hilltop and told the feds and sheriffs who wanted to arrest him on a gun charge—some pretty minor thing—to stick it. A siege started and the people doing the sieging made some unfortunate decisions, and the whole thing ended really badly. Shots were exchanged, and Weaver's unarmed and innocent wife and son were killed by a government sharpshooter; a federal marshal also died before the firing ended.

The second "issue" that the Sons were hot about was that other armed standoff between federal agents from the Bureau of Alcohol, Tobacco, and Firearms and the members of the Branch Davidian religious cult near Waco, Texas. It ended even more horribly, with the cult's compound going up in flames and a whole bunch of people, including women and children, dying.

A lot of people believe that anger at what happened in Waco led to the bombing of that federal building in Oklahoma City, where even more innocent people were slaughtered.

"The Sons use Ruby Ridge and Waco," Cam explained, "to prove that the federal government is waging a campaign against the rights and freedoms of ordinary Americans—us 'little guys.'"

"I don't know," I said. I pulled my feet out of the brook and walked over to flop down near the others. "It seems to me all they prove is that everyone makes mistakes. There doesn't have to be some big *conspiracy* going on. Federal agents are 'ordinary Americans,' too. Couldn't it just be a few guys screwing up?"

"Well, you may think that," Cam said, "and I may think that, but they don't. So to them, something like the Brady Bill is more of the same. They say the government wants to take away the people's right to bear arms—which is in the Constitution."

Millie snorted. "That's a bunch of crap," she said. "The Brady Bill doesn't take away anything. We've got a cousin back home who's a cop. He's also a big deer hunter and gun collector. But he said he and all his buddies on the force are a hundred percent behind the Brady Bill. They're for anything that makes it harder for guys with records to buy handguns."

"It's the same with that assault rifle ban," I put in. "Cops and ordinary people are all for it. That's what all the polls say." I was trying to dry my feet with my hands and get the pine needles off them.

"Look," said Cam. But he didn't look at me, or anyone. "It isn't me who's saying that conspiracy stuff." He was scrunching up his nose as if it itched or as if he didn't want to sneeze.

He took his big knife out of its sheath, and after brushing the pine needles off the ground in front of him, he began—if you can believe this—to play tick-tack-toe against himself.

"What you have to realize is...these guys, they all learned gun stuff from their dads." He sounded agitated. "Those dads, they took them out when they were kids and taught them how to hunt. They did that for the sake of meat, and sport, and getting off—*you* know, away. Out of the house, that kind of thing. And also, now they say, like, let's suppose there's someone breaking down your door, the entrance to your *castle*, and all that. It's only human nature to protect yourself, right? And a fella has to have a gun for that." He paused. "It can be argued."

Up to that point Michelle hadn't said anything, but now she looked at Cam and said, "That's what Honeycutt and them are doing, isn't it? Protecting themselves—they think. That's the reason for the sign and all that looking out the window. They're protecting themselves, aren't they? From what, though?"

Cam took a deep breath and with the back of his knife erased his tick-tack-toe games.

"Oh, let's see," he said. "The thing you must remember is that they've got their *passions*." He nodded to himself. "That'd be a good way of putting it. They've got passions—so they only see one side of anything. It isn't that they're...unintelligent." He rubbed a hand across his mouth. He looked like someone trying to figure something out. When he started talking again, his eyes were actually on Meesh.

"Look. All they want—who doesn't? We've talked about this—is to have things, to run things, like they want, in their own way," he said. "To have their rights and freedoms. On their land, especially. *You* know what I mean. Hey, that's what I want too—to just be left alone. Me, I'm close to being just the same as them...." He kind of left that hanging.

"Except...?" said Meesh.

"Except *what*?" said Cam. Now he'd looked back at the ground and was making a little furrow in the dirt with the point of his knife. It was about two feet long, going straight in her direction.

"I don't know," she said. "You tell me. You're just the same as them except for *something*. What?"

Cam laid down his knife and appeared to think it over. "If you *must* know," he finally said, "there are a couple of things. Just stupid stuff. Just talk on their part, mostly." He gave a little laugh. "Art likes to get them all riled up, I think. He likes it when he can get them going—Fred and Jess and Sandy. Me, that stuff is water off my back, his talk about some big ol' ruckus coming."

"Some *what?*" said Meesh. And then, "What kind of ruckus?"

"Art likes to say the U.N.'s taking over," said my brother with another little nervous laugh. He picked up his knife again and made another little furrow, this one crossing the first, and going from in front of Millie to in front of me. "He says the feds are giving the U.N. guys—these one-world folks—control of our country. He says the U.S. of A. is going to end up being run by Jews and foreigners, and that taking away our rights is step one in the establishment of this new world order. He believes that people are already being put in concentration camps here on our own soil. And that the rest of us, while we're still free, had better get together and resist. That's the big ol' ruckus—us against those other people. And it'll be hell because the other people will outnumber us."

"Like who? What 'other people'?" Michelle asked. "And who's that 'us' you're talking about?"

"Oh, *you* know." Cam made a vague gesture with his free hand. He hadn't made eye contact with anyone during his last "explanation." "The 'other people' would be most all the different immigrants, I guess—which would include all the blacks. Art says they all have many more kids than we do, on the average. He says minorities outnumber us already in a lot of places. Like in all the major cities. Taxes for their welfare are bleeding us white, he says, except we're white already." That laugh again. "That's who 'us' is, according to Art, ordinary Christian white people."

"Is that so?" said Meesh. "And where does that leave us natives? Maybe we'd say *Art* is the immigrant around here. But to him we're just another minority, right?"

136

"I know," said Cam, and he sighed. He leaned forward and with his knifepoint put the letter C on the end of the furrow nearest him, and an M at the end in front of Michelle.

"I've just been saying what Art says," he went on. "I've told him that the fact is, we whites stole all the land in North *and* South America. But he doesn't like to think of it that way. I don't believe he sees Native Americans as a problem, though. It's more the Jews and the blacks and the Mexicans and the Asians. Anyone that's got a funny name, he says."

"But wait," I said. "You don't believe that kind of racist garbage. You're no bigot, Cam." I was remembering back when he was so passionate about economic and educational equality for all, his "We Shall Overcome" period.

I was getting a little jumpy, if you want to know the truth. It was my brother's manner that had started me feeling that way—the sort of nervous, semi-but-not-totally apologetic tone in his voice when he was telling us about the Sons and the way they looked at things. That wasn't Cam's way. He'd taught me "common knowledge," like the right way to shake hands or to treat women; he wasn't into shilly-shallying or giving equal time to other points of view, not when it came to right-and-wrong issues like racism.

"Me?" he said now. "A bigot? No, of course I'm not. You know I love every person equally. As well as every animal and plant, all living things. And God, of course. I don't go in for politics." He laughed. "Or economics either. Taxes? I don't have to pay them—I don't have a job or any property, just the money that comes in from Dad, and that's all taken care of—deducted from, I guess you call it—before I even see it." He sobered up again. "But Art's got worries on account of taxes. He's fighting

137

with the government about his spread here, who owns it and all that."

"How do you mean?" asked Meesh.

Cam didn't answer right away. Instead he drew a C on my end of the other furrow and an M at Millie's end. And then he drew a circle around the two crossing lines he'd made, and those two C's and two M's at the ends of them. He nodded when he'd finished doing that, and I decided that he'd drawn a picture of the world he'd like to live in, a world with just two couples in it. How he'd guessed that Millie and I were on the way to becoming a couple, I can't tell you. I think I've heard that mentally unstable people often have, like, extrasensory perceptions. I don't know. Maybe what he'd drawn was just a doodle.

"I'm not sure," he finally said to Meesh. "Taxes figure in. Art's putting by a lot of food and clothes and fuel and medical supplies. And he's got some livestock, too. Maybe he thinks they're going to cut him off, or maybe he's going to cut *himself* off. At least for the time being, until the ruckus starts. That's what he's hinting at. He says that if they don't bother him, he won't bother them. Sometimes he says he's got a little independent state set up, right here, right now. With its own laws and courts and officials and everything. But I think that's just a joke of his. He likes to say the sheriff's already been tried and found guilty— and how he can barely wait to lock him up."

"Well, what he's saying *sounds* like a joke, all right," I said. "What's he want to do? Make this like the Middle Ages or something? He'd be King Arthur, right? And pretty soon he'd probably start a war with the next king down the road." Art's ideas seemed like such utter bullshit. This was the *United* States, for God's sake.

Cam sighed again. "I'm sort of too *busy* to think about that stuff," he said. "I have my own stuff going on. And it seems a whole lot more important than...well, anything. Here nobody bothers me. I can go off alone into the wilderness. I can...commune. I see amazing sights. And hear...the wisdom of the ages. From the source of it all."

He looked at me and smiled the most serene and gentle smile. Then he turned to Meesh and said, "Maybe I can talk to Art, and he'll allow you to stay here with me. And Chris and Millie, too. I think I could convince him. He respects me. I believe they all do."

I'd been trying to smile back at Cam, but I hate to think of how my face probably looked at that moment. There was a whole lot of jumble in my mind.

I'd just listened to my brother say he heard and saw things the rest of us (normal people?) couldn't see.

I'd also just heard my brother suggest that we all stay right here with him.

I'd hated hearing both those things. I'd hated having it (finally) come out of his own mouth that he was hallucinating, which made him—what?—a schizophrenic? And of course his suggestion that we all stay with the Sons of Liberty Two was unthinkable.

But I knew it wouldn't be smart for me to argue that point right then, at just that moment. Cam had made his suggestion because he *loved* us—and simply wasn't able to understand what a terrible idea that was. I could only hope that Meesh and Millie were cool and wouldn't say anything... provocative.

I turned my head to look at Meesh. She was my main worry.

139

In the last bunch of days, I'd found out her state of mind was changeable, to say the least.

Well, she was nodding and smiling at Cam, cool as could be; that was good. And slowly she put out her hand to him, palm down.

He took it, still with that serene expression on his face, then bent his head to kiss it.

chapter 22

We walked back to Sons of Liberty Two in pairs, Cam and Meesh (yes, holding hands), followed at a discreet distance by Millie and me. My idea was to keep them in sight (much as I respected— *believed in*—Cam's tracking skills, I didn't want to put them to the test) but to stay quite out of earshot. It was none of my beeswax—a saying of my mother's—what they talked about, just as what we said was none of theirs.

Millie felt pretty much the way I did about the rekindling— if you could call it that—of our siblings' romance. It was weird: the two of us, I realized, sounded almost like parents talking about the other two. I guess that's one of the side effects of mental illness: having other people, even younger ones, think they know more about what's good for you than you do. Probably too many people treat the mentally ill as if they're children all the time, just because they're trying to "protect" them from "mistakes" they think they might otherwise make. For example, if I'd found it necessary, I would have told my brother he was much better off with Michelle than with the perfidious Lisa. I'd have *pushed* him toward Michelle. How that would be in the long run wouldn't (didn't) concern me; right now was all I cared about. And right now I liked the sight of those two "kids" holding hands.

But I think the thing I liked most about this second part of our afternoon hike was how it felt being more or less alone with Millie.

The simple truth seemed to be that I had never been as comfortable—as *confident*—with anyone before. Maybe you know that feeling I'm talking about, where you just don't worry about…oh, being *judged* in any kind of negative way. Not that I was going to do this, but it seemed I could tell her about—for instance—my father's illness and his death, and how those things had made me feel. In other words, I wouldn't have been ashamed to cry in front of her. And at the same time I realized I was so confident of my feelings *about* her that it was now totally unimportant what my brother's—or my mother's—opinion of her might turn out to be. I knew, and that was all that mattered.

I think I may have become—if I've got the right word here—a little giddy.

By the time Art's compound came into view, my scheming rascal brain was trying to think of ways I might get back into some nearby woods, alone with her.

As soon as we entered the main house, I got a sense that whatever had transpired in our absence had gone well. Maybe they'd gotten good news about something—those problems Art'd been having about his taxes or whatever it was. In any event, when we walked in, you'd have thought we were the Prize Patrol with the $10 million check, or at least a brand-new Jaguar coupe in British racing green.

"Hey, it's about time, travelers!" Art Honeycutt hollered out, but wreathed in smiles to let us know he wasn't really mad. "We was afraid our buddy Cam had got you treed by some ol' grizzly." He raised a calming hand. "Not that we got 'em around here yet—"

"Far as we *know*," said Sandy Prime with that wink of his and a sly smile. "You never can tell what-all's out there nowadays. I swear I saw a wolf-dog not that long ago."

"Speakin' of which," said Art, "we thought we'd maybe wolf us down some steaks tonight. How does that sound? Have a little barbecue—turn Jesse loose on that new grill the boys picked up today. But before he gets that started, maybe you travelers'd like to get your things out of that car down there. And also you could grab a shower if you cared to. Some of us did that ourselves." He laughed. "It's not every day we get company."

"Especially good-lookin' company," said Sandy, and I could see that his long hair was still damp and that he had on rather different clothes—a polo shirt and a pair of chino slacks and instead of work boots, thongs.

"Like us to bring up our sleeping bags?" asked Meesh.

"Excellent idea," said Art. "I'm not sure the *maid* got any bunks made up this morning. And I gave her off tonight." The guys all laughed at that one.

Three quarters of an hour later we'd hauled up our stuff, been shown the bunkhouse (where Millie and Michelle had laid their sleeping bags on beds), everybody'd showered, and we'd all convened on the deck that opened off the back of the kitchen. On it, in addition to the big gas grill, were another picnic table with benches and a stack of dark green resin chairs. We each took one of those and sat around while Jesse, with some help from Fred and

Art, got dinner ready. Sandy said he wasn't going to cook ("Lucky thing for you guys") but that he'd get everybody knives and forks and plates and drinks and napkins—and he'd lend a hand with the cleanup later on. He said that with another of his annoying little winks.

Even before the meal was under way, I knew I was in one of those situations I guess everybody's been in at one time or another, where you find yourself making conversation with a bunch of people you don't know and are pretty sure you don't *want* to know. But at the same time you're trying to make a halfway decent impression on them? I thought Meesh and Millie did a better job of acting natural than I did—they must have gotten Meesh's medication just exactly right. It seemed to me that I kept sounding forced and insincere. Sitting in my uncomfortable resin chair, I kept trying to dry my sweaty palms by rubbing them discreetly on my denimed thighs.

When the food was ready, it was good—as well as being a welcome distraction—and there was plenty of it: T-bone steaks and mounds of French fries and stacks of sweet corn. For once I didn't feel at all self-conscious about how much I ate; this guy Jesse could really pack it in—I think he had eight ears of corn, and they were big ones. All of us new arrivals babbled compliments at him, and that got him grinning and bobbing his big head up and down. He and his buddies were all knocking back cans of beer, but Cam doesn't drink anything alcoholic so I didn't either, and neither did the girls. Cam had water and the rest of us had some store-brand cola. What with all the excitement and the exercise and the clean country air, a couple of beers might have put me right on my ass and made me look like an even bigger jerk than I did sober. Much as I'd have liked to drink a beer for relaxation reasons, I really didn't dare take the chance.

It was during my attack on a second big T-bone that Art reintroduced the question of our stay, the length of it, etc.

"What I've been thinking..." he began. "What we've *all* been thinking," he amended, "is that the three of you should plan to roost right here with us for three-four days—right up until the week*end*, say. No point, seeing as you're partway settled in, for you to get all packed again and go to a motel. We wouldn't feel right having you do that. And seeing as you drove so far for the privilege"—he chuckled—"it's only right that you should visit with ol' Cam awhile."

That caught me by surprise, his saying that, and I popped another big piece of steak into my mouth before he finished, so I wouldn't have to answer right away. Chewing hard, I stole a glance at Millie just in time to see her look at me. Of course, I thought I knew what she was thinking. Just what I was: This might complicate my plan to get Cam out of there. But still, what could we say but "Thanks a lot" and "Fine and dandy"?

Michelle became our spokesperson. "We wouldn't want to put you out," she said. "Much as we'd *like* to stay."

"Hey, no problem," Art informed her. "Be good for us to have some houseguests. Might make us mind our manners."

(*"Right,"* somebody muttered—and it wasn't either of the girls or Cam or me.)

"Well, I hope at least you'll let us help out with the cooking," the ever-cheerful Meesh replied.

"And could it be you're also into doing dishes?" Sandy asked in a seriously kidding tone of voice.

"Me, I'm scared to *death* of getting dishpan hands," said

Jesse Brink, clowning it up, holding up both palms in mock alarm.

"Hell, I got a load or two of wash you girls could do," Fred Slocum volunteered, getting into the spirit of things.

I guess those comments prompted Millie and Meesh to get up and start collecting plates and serving dishes. Sandy went with them into the kitchen and after a while came back with a half-gallon of butterscotch ripple ice cream, along with spoons and bowls. He was shaking his head and chuckling.

Art then asked me what route we'd taken, driving out. I thought he was just being polite, but after I answered—not in great detail—all the other guys (except Cam) jumped right in, and pretty soon there was a general conversation going on about ways to get from one place to another, and everybody (other than Cam) told some highway experience that he'd had somewhere— apparently they'd all done lots of driving (trucks and "pleasure cars"), even as far east as Pennsylvania, it turned out. You've probably noticed how much most middle-aged men seem to like to talk about their cars and stuff that's happened to them driving. Maybe I'll get to be like that when I get older, but right now...well, I'm not turned on at all by my—or anybody else's— automotive life. But at least their interest in this subject meant I didn't have to think of things to say.

Art had just—finally—changed the subject to Pat Buchanan (who he'd heard give "a hell of a speech" on one of those car trips of his, and who he wished had gotten to be president) when Meesh and Millie rejoined the gents and told us they'd just about fallen asleep at the sink and now were ready for their bunks. And when Cam announced it was his bedtime, too, I quickly said I'd join him.

146

Jesse sat there expressionless. I had the feeling that he wouldn't miss us.

"It's time for me to have another beer," was all Fred Slocum said.

As we left I made myself a bet that those ice cream bowls and spoons would still be on the deck—or *maybe* in the sink—come morning.

When I was six years old, the year our father died, Cam'd let me sleep in the extra bed in his room sometimes, but I don't believe I've ever slept in the same room with him since—up until that night. Come to think of it, I don't believe I've slept in the same room with *anyone* during the past eleven years.

So it was sort of awkward but also kind of nice undressing and getting into bed with my brother right there. And it gave me a chance to ask him something Millie and I had wondered about.

"When you were telling us about the different things that Art and them are storing up," I said, "you didn't say anything about guns. I saw a few downstairs in that cabinet he has, but you mentioned how these guys grew up with guns, and Art did tell us all those hunting stories. So it kind of surprised Millie and me that they wouldn't stock up on guns and ammunition if they were— like you said—thinking that they might be cut off from supplies."

"Funny you should mention that," said Cam, "'cause that happens to be something I've been talking to Art about a lot— the whole gun culture. What I've been after him to do—him and the others—is to sort of wean themselves away from firearms. And into bows and arrows." He smiled benignly. "It shouldn't be that hard for them to do. They already do some bow hunting, and they all like it. The difficult part—as I mentioned before—is that guns are part of their heritage. And a kind of *habit*, you could say. Like cracking your knuckles."

It was hard to imagine Cam telling older guys like Fred Slocum and Jesse Brink that using a gun was like cracking a knuckle; it was equally hard to imagine him telling them to do *anything*. They were going to listen to some punk kid who ran around in short pants? But I wasn't about to argue the point. Apparently my poor deluded brother seemed to think he'd had some sort of useful dialogue with them.

"So you don't believe they've added to their gun collection— just in case they need some extras someday?" I inquired, trying to sound as if I didn't care.

"No, I'm pretty sure they haven't," he said. "I have the run of all the storage places, so I'd know. But the main thing is that Art's been pretty heavily exposed to my thinking on the subject of firearms. I don't believe he'd go against my wishes."

That sounded *really* delusional to me. I mean, for Cam to think his "wishes" mattered to a man like Arthur Honeycutt...How long had he even known Art Honeycutt? A week? Ten days? And Art did not believe my brother got his wishes straight from God—he'd made that pretty clear, I thought.

"He's seen what I can do," my brother added.

"How d'you mean?" I said.

Cam smiled and shook his head. He seemed a little...I don't know...embarrassed.

"I've performed a few illusions for the guys," he said. "Magic tricks—*you* know. A lot with cards at first—them seeming to change their spots, and so on. But then some other ones, too."

"Like what?" I said.

"I changed some bullets into bean seeds," Cam told me. "Right before their very eyes. It took some prep beforehand—but they're pretty gullible, not the most sophisticated audience I've ever seen. And I gave the routine a biblical spin: the swords into plowshares bit. I said I didn't want them bringing in more guns and ammunition, that if they did, I'd have to change them into seeds and shovels. The guns they have down in the cabinet are enough, I told them."

"And they seemed to go along with that?" I asked him.

"I think," my brother said. And then he smiled again. "They'd better." And on that cryptic note he reached for the light switch. "Time to get some sleep. Good night, dear *frater*."

I told him to sleep tight. Then I shut up; I didn't want to ask him why "they'd better" and start a whole new conversation. The thing was, I still had plans for the evening. I wanted him to fall asleep fast, so I could sneak out and head over to the bunkhouse. No, not to invite Millie to take an evening stroll in the woods. I wanted to talk strategy with her and Meesh.

Art's invitation, which had sounded almost like an insistence that we stay right where we were for another three or four days, definitely concerned me. I'd been thinking that if we checked into a motel, we could have gotten Cam off the compound without arousing his or anyone else's suspicions. It would have been easy and natural to say we wanted to show him the place we were staying and to treat him to a meal at a restaurant we were pretty sure he'd like. Then once we had him off the grounds, we could tell him something we'd decided on beforehand that would convince him to keep on going with us. Ever since our hike, I'd figured Meesh might be the one who could convince him to do...well, almost anything.

But it had sounded to me as if Art hadn't wanted any of us going anywhere. Could he have guessed what we had in mind and was determined to keep an eye on us? Or was I just being paranoid? It seemed downright peculiar to me that in a matter of a few hours he'd changed his mind from wanting to be rid of us real quick to serving us steak dinners and urging us to hang around.

I didn't for a moment believe that Cam's sleight-of-hand magic had convinced Art and the others that he had supernatural powers. Those guys might be idiots, but they watched TV and this wasn't the Dark Ages when everyone believed in sorcery. No, I had to think Art had a better reason for not giving Cam the old hee-haw when he threatened to turn their shootin' irons into garden spades.

What I needed to do really badly, it seemed to me, was to talk all this over with Millie and Meesh. I tried to make my breathing regular and will my brother into dreamland.

chapter 23

I saw Cam do his "cat thing."

Well, I *think* I did. Or maybe he was just...being considerate of me, trying not to wake his little brother.

I might have fallen asleep—that's what I'm not sure about. I *think* I was just lying there with my eyes closed, taking slow deep breaths, trying to get Cam to fall asleep—but it could be that I put myself out first. But in any case, all of a sudden my eyes were slitted open, and I was seeing Cam go sort of *sliding* off his bed. After that, he stretched—on all fours on the floor, he was—then quick as a wink he's balanced on the sill of our wide-open window. Another wink and he's not there. If I heard him land—oh, ten feet down—it was just barely.

Well. Clearly I was not the only one with other plans for the evening. Maybe Cam and I had the same thing in mind: a conversation with the girls. Or maybe he'd set something up with Meesh earlier and now had left to meet her. Possibly—I hated to admit this—he (that is, his "cat" persona) had just gone hunting. In his shorts. For mice or chipmunks or whatever.

I got out of bed and put some clothes on, everything but socks and shoes; I carried those. At the window I looked out, but only to refresh my memory. It *was* about a ten-foot drop, not suitable for someone of my bulk and disposition. No (I told myself), I'd have to exit more conventionally.

I stepped out onto the second-floor landing, closing our room door behind me. Lights were on downstairs, and I could hear voices coming from the deck. That meant at least two of our hosts were still up. But it also meant that with them outside I could exit through the front door without them seeing me. I just had to hope that no one would come in to get another beer while I was scampering across the living room.

My luck was good: Nobody saw me. When I was safe outside the door, I stopped and took a minute to let my eyes adjust to the comparative darkness. It wasn't pitch-black out—not with about a million stars and half a moon all shining. Even I, no cat for sure, could see shapes of trees and other stuff quite clearly.

Now I had a choice to make, I realized. I couldn't simply take the short walk to the bunkhouse—the deck came off the house in that direction, and anybody sitting on it would be sure to spot me. So I could either hang around and wait for the guys to go to bed, or I could angle away from both buildings and make a huge half-circle through unknown territory that would eventually bring me around to the other side of the bunkhouse.

When I remembered there'd been talk of wolves and bears that day, I decided I could wait quite happily. So *Where?* became the question.

At once two things occurred to me. First, I'd really like to know what guys like Art and Jesse and Fred *talked* about when they were by themselves. (Would it be stock-car racing? The merits and demerits of Garth Brooks and k.d. lang? Or maybe what kind of fence "we" ought to build along the Mexican and Canadian borders?) And second, if I moved along right up against the wall of the house until I got almost to the corner, I could sit down and be in a pretty good position to overhear just about anything they said. The deck, you see, was narrower than the house by a good bit, and centered off the kitchen end. So it'd be impossible for anyone on it to see a person where I planned to be. All I had to do was get there quietly.

And this I did, using a modified version of Cam's stalking technique. I felt like a bit of an idiot, doing that slow goose step in the dark—but, hey, it worked. And I was able to tune into their conversation right away.

"Gone and got the hots for them damn 'breeds," was what I first heard clearly: the surly sound of Mr. Slocum speaking.

"So?" No question: Sandy Prime. "You see that nice rack on the little one? No bra or nothin', right? Sweet as royal Riviera pears, they'd be. Don't think I didn't grab some ass when they was doin' dishes, man."

"Yeah? And what'd *they* do?" Fred wanted to know.

"Wiggled some, is all," said Sandy. "They said to cut it out, but I know they liked it. I'll give 'em something they *really* like before they go, I betcha."

"I think *he's* a fruit," Jesse grunted. So there were three out there.

"Who? Which one? The brother?" Fred now asked.

"No—*him*. Our Mister Short Pants. Cammie-boy."

"Could be," said Sandy thoughtfully. "He's got a lot of *queer* ideas." He chuckled.

"He better watch himself if he comes sniffin' around *me*,"

153

said Jesse. A few beers seemed to have washed away his earlier cheerfulness. "I'd break the little shit in two."

"*Look.*" That was Art Honeycutt all of a sudden. I'd been thinking that he wasn't out there. "Everybody cut the crap, okay?" He sounded pissed, cold sober. "You know the guy's a fuckin' gold mine. Christ almighty, you forget already what you got today? Paid for by whose money? He's like a gift from God, is what he is."

"I like my gifts shaped different and with attitude," Sandy let him know. "Then unwrapping them's like half the fun." He laughed again.

"You gotta unwrap something, get your ass to town," Art told him. "Just keep your hands off them two sisters. That's all we need, him getting pissed and closing up the vault on us."

There were sounds like someone getting up and crossing the deck.

"Sometimes I think your brain's between your legs, I swear," said Art, and I could hear his footsteps leaving, walking through the kitchen. The population of the deck was down to three.

"Screw him," said Sandy, but not loudly. And when he went on, he was mumbling. "Just 'cause he don' want to…Have a little fun, is all. Why, hell, I know them 'breeds would love to…."

"Me, I gotta piss," said Jesse Brink.

I heard four thudding footsteps, then a zipper going down. Moments later a heavy stream from above splashed onto the ground no more than ten feet from the place I sat hugging my knees.

When it stopped, there was another zipper sound and those same footsteps now retreating. Then came a heavy belch.

"Well. I guess I'll hit the sack," big Jesse said.

"Can't put off tomorrow," said Fred the philosopher. A chair scraped back.

"Nothin' else to do around this goddamn place," said Sandy.

Someone crushed a beer can in his hand and dropped it on the deck; someone else tossed an empty one out into the darkness. A lot of footsteps crossed the kitchen and went up the stairs. I listened hard for a couple of minutes; I was pretty sure they had all left the deck. I decided that I'd give it ten more minutes, though, before I moved. Let them settle down up there. It was 11:48 on my digital wristwatch.

I had a lot to think about, for sure. I'd forgotten all about Cam's money. Each and every month he received the same amount that I did from our father's estate, and it was possible—even likely—he hadn't spent a dime at Gramercy Manor. He also didn't own a car, nor did he spend much on his wardrobe, ever. Quite probably the guy was loaded. Or had been, depending on how much he'd handed over to Art Honeycutt. No wonder he'd said "They'd better" when we were talking about the Sons going along with his gun policies. He thought that he—or his money, anyway—could make them toe the line. Instead, I now believed, the opposite had happened.

I decided that I had to take a look around the compound—or at least a part of it—before I went on to the bunkhouse. I was thinking about that load the guys had picked up while we were on our hike—a hike suggested by Art Honeycutt, as I recalled. He probably wanted to make sure Cam didn't see what they brought back, not barbecue grills and stuff like that but a load of guns, most likely. If I could find them, that'd give me leverage to talk my brother out of there.

So when my ten minutes were up, I put on my shoes and socks and rubbed some life back into my cramped legs. Then, still stepping softly, I headed for the biggest storage area they had, the one that Cam had called the barn.

I entered it through an ordinary half-glass door a short ways down from a huge pair of heavy wooden sliding doors—old-fashioned barn doors is what they were, of course. Once inside I wished I had a flashlight. About the only thing I could see at all was the white Honda Michelle'd lent to Cam parked to the right of where I was, on the main floor of the barn. And when I felt my way past it, I came upon a big delivery van—perhaps the very vehicle they'd used to get the guns.

Though it seemed like a bit of a long shot, I decided that I'd see if I could get inside the back of it, on the off chance that they hadn't had time to unload before we got back. Later on, I realized what an absurd idea that was: What did I expect to find, a pile of assault rifles lying around on the van's floor? Suppose I'd found some packing crates. What would I have used to open them, my teeth?

That never got to be an issue. The van had nothing in it. When I came out, I groped my way to where I'd started and then took a few more steps in the opposite direction. What I found was box stalls, or at least *one* box stall. It had one of those double cottage doors on it, with only the bottom half closed, but of course I couldn't see inside it. I did lean in and sniff, however, and I thought there *possibly* might be an animal in there. I hesitated, then convinced myself that no matter what was in there, it almost surely wasn't loose guns and ammunition. This was stupid, I decided; I was wasting time. Maybe the girls would have a flashlight I could borrow later. I should get back to my original plan and head for the bunkhouse.

It wasn't far away—oh, maybe 150 feet at most—and when I got closer to it, I could see a light still on inside. Get the picture: I was walking toward the *end* of the bunkhouse—the main door was on one side—and its windows were all above eye level, perhaps because of all the double-decker bunks in there, angled against the walls. So what I saw through a couple of open windows was some little bits of bunkhouse ceiling, illuminated by what I guessed would be a forty- or sixty-watt bulb.

And when I got really close, I could just barely hear a voice inside, a guy's voice talking softly in a kind of breathy whisper. Of course I figured it was Cam's.

"*So beautiful…*" I heard. "Since I first laid eyes on you…" I stopped to listen better, feeling a little out of place but also interested. My brother the makeout artist! "Never had a feeling for a girl like this before…"

But then there came a girl's voice, unmistakably Millie's, and she was talking louder, sounding stressed.

"No, really. Cut it out," she said. "I'm going to holler if you don't…I swear."

For an instant there I thought: What's going on? Cam hitting on my Millie? Where's Meesh, for God's sake?

But then I heard the guy's voice once again, and clearer.

"You holler and you'll get big Jesse down here, babe. And I can *guarantee* you won't like what *he*'ll want to do…"

Ye Christ, I thought. Sandy Prime was in there!

chapter 24

It isn't often that I do something important without thinking, at all. Quite possibly this was the first time ever; before I left my house with Meesh and Millie, I did *pause* a moment.

Or maybe I *did* think first. Maybe you have to. Maybe if you don't, you can't do anything. That makes a certain amount of sense.

So maybe what I really mean is that I didn't *consider* what to do. I'm pretty sure—positive, in fact—that I didn't say to myself, "Well, Chris, there are a number of possible courses of action you might follow here. For one, you *could* do this, but that might lead to such-and-such, so you'd probably be better off—*everyone* would be—if you made a different choice. Such as…" and so on. There wasn't any of that.

No, when I realized Sandy Prime was inside the bunkhouse doing something to Millie, I just moved. I started running—fast, I guess. It seemed like I was really motoring, with my feet hardly touching the ground. But that's pretty unlikely; I'm a load, as you know. In fact, I probably sounded like a herd of elephants once I was inside the bunkhouse and running down the middle of this one big room, avoiding the woodstove in the aisle between those double-decker bunks.

I'm pretty sure I was quiet in one respect, though: I don't believe I said, or shouted, anything. Not something classical, like "Unhand that woman, you swine!" or the more informal "Let go of her, you son of a bitch!" or the extremely simple, basic "Ki–i–i–ll!"

I just pounded into that building going as hard as I could and, as the saying goes, saving my breath. I imagine that's the way a lion goes when it's running down a zebra, say. It just digs in and goes flat out, and when it gets close, it pounces.

That's what I did, anyway. As soon as I was through the door, I saw the fix that Prime had Millie in. She was on a lower bunk, up at the head of it, not flat on the mattress but leaning back, her upper body partly supported by a pillow and the wall. Prime was on top of her but not *lying* on top of her. He was kind of sitting on the bunk with his body twisted around and bent over her; his feet were still on the floor. Even in the dim light I could plainly see that Millie had on a big lilac-colored T-shirt and black bikini underpants.

She was doing her best to fight off Prime, to push him away, but he had his right hand way up underneath her T-shirt and was trying to collect her wrists with his left. And he appeared to be trying to kiss her. She was making little struggle sounds.

When I got to them, I didn't hesitate. I simply put both hands around Prime's neck and squeezed. And started backing up and pulling—dragging him away from her.

He didn't come too easily at first, because that one hand of his got sort of tangled up inside her shirt. But that was also good in that it meant he only had his left, at first, to try and hit me with. And by the time he'd freed the other one, his right, his air supply had been cut back awhile, and he wasn't capable of doing

159

me much harm. My hands—and all the rest of me, in fact—are pretty strong, remember.

And I was in a zone, of course. I'm sure adrenaline had much to do with this whole scene. My system must have been just flooded by the stuff, and Sandy Prime, at the time when I first put the clutch on him, probably had that part of his factory shut down. The last thing you expect, I suppose, when you're forcing yourself on a woman, is to find you're being choked to death from behind. It doubtless also helped that he was partly drunk and not coordinating all that well.

Once he was free of her, I kept on backing up and dragging him. I noticed little details: one of his thongs had come off, and his hair was now completely dry. I imagine I was hating him, and maybe I was still afraid of him. I didn't kid myself. I knew if Sandy Prime and I had seven fights, he'd win six of them. But this wasn't any series starting here; if I had anything to do with it, this was one game only.

Eventually—I'm sure it took a little while—Millie's cries got through to me.

"Chris, let go!" I heard. "You're going to kill him!"

And so I might have, if she hadn't brought me to—as they say—"my senses." I let go of Sandy's throat. His head dropped down and hit the floor, making quite a thud. It seemed as if he was hanging on the edge of consciousness just barely; he wasn't well at all. I looked down at him and didn't feel the least bit sorry. All I felt was hatred and contempt.

I turned to Millie. "You okay?" I said. "He didn't…hurt you, did he?"

Call me crude, or just observant, but it had already registered on me that no one's pants were off, or even open.

"No," said Mil. "I'm fine. He only...just got here."

I stood beside her and we stared at Sandy Prime. You could see his eyes begin to focus. He struggled to sit up and touched his throat. I wondered if I'd crushed or broken something in that area. He tried to talk, but what came out was just some rasping sounds.

"Is there anything that you could get some water in?" I said to Mil. He looked really whipped, but I wasn't going to leave the two of them alone.

She went to the bathroom and came back with a paper cup, which she handed to him. He drank a little. I could see that it was hard for him to swallow.

"She asked me to come down," he croaked. "It was her idea."

I looked at Millie, not because I needed her denial, but more to show her that I knew the guy was lying.

"Try again," I said to Sandy Prime. "That's bullshit."

He took a deep breath and dropped his eyes. You could almost hear the wheels turning.

"I'd had some beers..." he started. "Musta lost my mind a little...." This came out in that same throaty whisper, fast. He kept fingering his Adam's apple and shaking his head. "Been cooped up out here so long, seein' a great-lookin' woman musta made me crazy....Really, really sorry. Not like me. Don' have to force myself on girls. No shit, not ever. We don' have to bring this up with...*you* know, Art. Now, do we? Or, like, Cam? They'd lose respect. I swear, I'll never, *ever*...swear to God."

It cost him saying that. He wasn't used to pleading. I could imagine how he hated being hurt by *me*, a punk kid from the East.

"That all's up to her," I told him. I figured that of course we'd tattle. Let Art kick the son of a bitch the hell off his property. Then I wouldn't have to watch my back when he felt better.

"I don't think we need to say anything," Millie said. "We'll be going soon. This can stay between the three of us."

I looked at her, amazed. I'd thought she'd stall, keep him in the dark, on edge.

He, however, looked delighted. Still seeming kind of woozy, he scrambled to his feet, coughing as he did so.

Millie caught my eye and gave me a "don't argue" look. It was the first time I'd seen her use it, though I've had it from my mom a hundred times at least. Maybe women just inherit it—like frizzy hair.

"Thanks a whole lot," Sandy rasped. He shook his head again. "Really, really sorry. No hard feelings, now. G'night." He left the bunkhouse, now a little bit bent over, still working on his throat.

I turned to Mil at once, of course, and wrapped my arms around her. We both were shaking, and I tried to counteract that by burying my face in the soft warm place where her neck meets her shoulder, and nuzzling around. She smelled delicious; we both soon settled down.

"Talk about *timely*," she finally said. She'd pulled back her head to look at me, but she kept her grip around my waist. "I was seriously scared. He thought I'd *welcome* him, the slimy bastard." Then teasingly, "Let's see—I can't remember. Is it *you* I asked to come down here?"

I couldn't get over how tough she was—how well she was taking this.

"I've known his type before, back home," she said. "I thought I could probably talk him out of...*you* know—*it*. But I wasn't sure how drunk he was. That had me worried. I told him we wouldn't say anything so he'd know his buddies weren't going to hear about it. Guys like him are all image. This way he won't feel he has to, like, get even."

I took her word on that; I didn't know Prime's "type" at all, I guess. It seemed to me he still might feel he owed me... *something*. Yet I knew he had extra reasons for not wanting Cam to know anything about this incident. That was one of the things I wanted to talk to Mil about.

"Okay," I said. "So where's Meesh, anyway?"

"Somewhere with Cam," she told me. "He showed up a while ago, and off they went. She knew that he was coming."

"How's she...doing, do you think?" I guess that was my subtle way of asking if her medication was still working well. I wanted to know how...*rational* she was—and would be in the morning.

"Good," said Millie. I think she'd read my mind. "She wants to get Cam out of here, now. In the beginning, she was blown away by how beautiful this place is, but that's all over with. She's seen and heard who these guys are. And she got groped by our friend, too—back there in the kitchen."

"Well, wait'll you hear this," I said. And I rattled off that stuff about Cam giving money to the group, and how I was pretty sure they'd used it to buy guns.

"Oh, you are, are you?" she said. "Well, come with me then, smarty."

She grabbed a flashlight from her backpack and led me down the aisle to the very end of the bunkhouse. There, she

163

climbed onto an upper bunk and, kneeling, raised both hands and pushed up on the ceiling. A piece of it gave way, and she shoved it to one side. There was storage space up there, an attic.

"Take a peek," she said.

I climbed up next to her. She handed me the light and I stuck my head and shoulders into the hole in the ceiling.

Oh, my. I guess it was the load they'd gone for, earlier that day. What I was looking at was labeled crates of weapons and boxes of ammunition. Not enough stuff to fight a war with maybe, but a lot more than four hunters would need.

"Does Meesh know about this?" I asked right away, also thinking: Does *Cam* know, by now?

"Unh-unh," said Millie. "We noticed the trapdoor when we brought our stuff up from the car. But then we got into taking showers and getting ready for the barbecue. And by the time we got back here, it was dark and we were tired, so we kind of just forgot about it. But after Cam came down and the two of them took off, I remembered and decided to investigate."

We closed the trapdoor and climbed down.

"I want to split tomorrow," I told her. "But without them getting suspicious ahead of time. Maybe we can just say we have to run into town to get something—I don't know what...."

"That's easy," Millie said. "Tampax. Jerks like these would never think to order any."

"Right," I said. "And we could also say that I had to get ... like, a prescription filled."

"We could even leave our sleeping bags behind," said Mil. "And Meesh's car—although I've kind of had my eye on it. But as long as we didn't pack up—you know?—they probably wouldn't think we're going to run off with their money man."

"Maybe we *can* take both cars," I said, "and tell them ours needs servicing. We can say we want to leave it for a tune-up and an oil change. But what worries me the most is Cam. If he'll go along with this whole idea, or not."

"Well, what do *you* think?" Millie asked. "He's your brother."

"I sort of think he will," I said. "I know he'll hate being taken advantage of. And he'll be furious when he hears about Prime hitting on you two. The only question is: What will he feel *he* ought to do? Will leaving be...*appropriate* for him? I don't know. He's pretty unpredictable; I mean, he always has been. He could flat refuse to run away. But if Meesh really wanted him to...."

I think Millie understood what I was saying: that a lot depended on how sick my brother was. The smartest thing for him to do—the *rational* thing—was to get the hell away from there. But Cam, looking through the filter of his illness, might not make that judgment.

"Well, I guess we'll have to wait and see," she said. She paused, looked up at me, and smiled. "But for right now, d'you think you'd like to stay here for a while?" I wasn't sure I'd seen that particular smile before on her.

I didn't have to think. Of course I wanted to stay. My mouth got kind of dry.

"For sure," I managed to get out.

She unzipped her sleeping bag and spread it, flannel side down, on the lower mattress.

"That can be our cover," she said. "But you should take your shoes off and...well, those jeans look kinda...rough."

Even a neophyte like me could take a hint like that. In a moment, both of us were dressed—undressed—the same, and on the bunk and tight together, head (or, make that lips) to toes.

And in a little while our kissing got a good bit more emphatic, and soon my hands went sliding underneath her shirt, enjoying what I'd almost killed a man for doing not that long ago.

She seemed to like that, making little purring sounds. We—both of us—were totally blissed out, I think. I know I'd never been so happy. In addition to being turned on, I just *appreciated* her so much, everything about her. There wasn't any need to hurry on to doing something else. What was happening just then seemed perfect.

I don't know if either of us ever considered the possibility of having Cam and Meesh arrive in the middle of all this. I'm pretty sure I didn't. What we were doing wasn't anything to be ashamed of. What I think we both felt was a lovely sense of rightness—how lucky we both were to have each other.

I don't believe I would've minded if my mother'd "caught us" then.

No, wait—I'm overdoing it.

chapter 25

It was starting to get light outside by the time I finally made it back to my brother's bedroom in the main house.

Here's the explanation: I'd decided to stay on in the bunkhouse until Cam and Meesh got back; I just wasn't going to leave Millie alone again until we were far, far away from the Sons of Liberty Two. Also, to tell you the truth, after—or maybe even during—all that kissing and fondling, the two of us fell fast asleep.

It was Michelle, alone, who woke us up, and almost as soon as she did, I was out of there. As I left, Millie was rattling on about the Sandy Prime attack, and Meesh was trying to interrupt her, but it didn't seem to me I had the time to hang around and listen. I didn't want the other goons to know that I'd been off the premises.

Cam seemed to be napping when I tiptoed into his room, but his eyes snapped open before I reached my bed.

"Where in God's name have you been?" he asked me, speaking very softly, just above a whisper. "I was worried."

I appreciated that; even in his present state he was my big bro, still looking after me.

"I was down at the bunkhouse with Millie," I told him.

167

"Michelle woke us up just a little bit ago. I've got a ton of stuff to tell you."

"I've got a lot to tell you, too," said Cam. He stayed under his blanket, lying on his side and staring wide-eyed at me. "Listen up: This place is totally surrounded. Totally. The entire hilltop is."

I forgot about undressing and sat down on the edge of my bed. I must admit my first thought was: He's raving. And had been hallucinating maybe.

"Right," I said. "By fields of wheat and barley. And by wolves. Just don't tell me it's United Nations forces." I smiled to show that I was trying to make a joke. Trying and failing, I realized; what I'd said was stupid and unfunny. Face it, I was overtired.

"No, you idiot," Cam said, but he didn't seem angry. "By the local sheriff and his deputies, and some state troopers. And some other ones in civvies. I'm not sure—they could be FBI."

"You're serious," I said. He definitely was, and I was pleased to find that I believed him now. "But how did you find out?"

He heaved a sigh. "I *saw* them, Chris," he said. "I was taking Michelle to a spot I wanted her to see, and we almost walked into one of their little groups. But they didn't see us or hear us, so I left her in a safe place and did a circuit of the hill. It's definitely a whatchamacallit—a *cordon*. No one can get in or out."

He sounded a bit excited saying that. I got *real* excited hearing it.

"They'd let *us* out," I said. "I'm sure they would. Let's go right now. Let's get the girls and split. We can take your car." I'd seen his keys on the dresser between our beds, and now I reached over, picked them up, and put them in my pocket.

"Hold on, hold on," said Cam. He hadn't moved. "Slow down there, buddy. You're saying that the four of us should go skulking away, under the cover of darkness, abandoning these guys? I don't think so. They took me in, don't forget—a stranger in a strange land. And we share, in many ways, a common vision."

"Is that so?" I said. It was time for him to hear about my evening's work and face some hard, unpleasant facts. "And does your common vision include attempted rape and stockpiling guns and ammunition?"

Talking fast, I gave him the whole story, just about—what I'd overheard and seen and (finally) had to do on Millie's behalf. I was blunt, sarcastic, undiplomatic—all of which I probably shouldn't have been—but I was in a hurry to get going, and I hoped to light a fire under Cam.

No such luck. Instead of leaping up, he frowned. But then he did, very slowly, *sit* up, shrugging off his blanket and dropping his feet onto the floor. He still had on the same green shorts, but the knife was off his belt; I noticed his bare feet were heavily callused. He put his elbows on his knees and bent way over, so as to scratch his head with both hands. He was doing everything in slo-mo.

"This is almost unbelievable," he said as he straightened up again. "There has to be some explanation. I can't believe these men are capable of... well, such perfidy. I'm not speaking of what Sandy did to Mil—that's something else. I think the man's an addict, a sexual compulsive; the urge is always with him—you should hear him talk. Satyriasis that's called. It came up in Abnormal Psych in college. It's also known as Don Juanism, if I remember right."

He was looking off into space, now on this other track, the "perfidy" of Art and them forgotten.

"Yes, Don Juanism," he continued. "I'm certain that's the name. Did you happen to see that Don Juan movie a couple of years ago? I think Antonio Banderas might've been in it, somebody like that. Maybe it was Christian Slater or...no, it was Johnny *Depp*, I'm almost positive. But what the heck was its name—the movie's *name*. It's almost on the tip of my tongue... hold on, I'm getting it—*Don Juan DeMarco*! Yes!" He looked at me triumphantly. The frown was long gone. Everything was cool. He'd remembered a movie title. That'll give you an idea of the kind of shape he was in.

"Look, Cam," I said. "The point is that these guys are screwballs and outlaws, and they're now armed to the teeth. Art *lied* to you about the whole gun issue, and he's used your money to stock a little armory up here. Doesn't it make sense to leave— and get the girls out—before we end up in the middle of a shoot-out?"

Cam's eyes came back to the here-and-now while I was saying that. But I could tell my reasonable tone hadn't had the desired effect. He sat there with a small smile on his face, slowly shaking his head.

"This may be hard for you to understand," he told me, using the patient cadence of a person who's explaining why the leaves change color to a child of two or three, "but I may be the very person who can keep it from *becoming* a shoot-out. I happen to possess, you see, the single most important attribute a mediator can have: I can—and *do*—sympathize with both sides in this confrontation."

I started to protest, wanting to say that he could do that just as well from the other side of the gate, but he, shaking his head some more, held up a silencing palm.

"On the one hand," he continued, "there's the sheriff's point of view—more than that, his *duty*. Art has received services from all levels of the government—whether he likes or wants the services or not. And he's refused to pay the taxes that support those services. So according to the law, it was correct for the authorities to sell his property on a tax foreclosure or whatever it's called, after so-and-so many years of nonpayment of taxes. And now it's up to the sheriff to order Art and the boys off the land."

"So how can you sympathize with Art?" I said. "He hasn't got a leg to stand on. He's defying the law. And on top of that, he's a hate-mongering racist and a proven liar."

"Ah," said Cam. "But I'm also able to look at things from Art's point of view. Beauty is in the eye of the beholder, don't forget. And Art's vision is, in many ways, quite beautiful."

"How can you *say* that?" I said. "He's—"

"*Because*," Cam cut me off, "like me, Art and the others want to form a partnership—a unity—with God. Putting some of their behavior to one side, these are basically religious people, Chris, in terms of their beliefs. Art told me where they're coming from one day when it was just the two of us. He sees himself and the other Sons—the three here and maybe a dozen others in the area—as Christian Israelites."

"As *what*?" I said. I was a long time out of Sunday school, but nothing that I'd heard Art say had sounded particularly Christian, and he'd flat-out labeled Jews—who are the only Israelites I'd ever heard of—as enemies of his, his oppressors.

"He believes they're all descended from the ten lost tribes of

Israel," said Cam. "This is in the Bible, you see—the book of Kings, I think Art said—where the Assyrians captured these folks when they conquered Palestine in the eighth century B.C. And there's evidence to support the claim that the tribes eventually migrated to England and northern Europe and settled there. Which means that all the white people whose ancestors came over here from that area are direct descendants of those old Israelites!"

"Wait," I said. "I took world history in junior high. I don't remember anything like that. He's saying all those Celts and Danes and stuff are descended from Abraham the prophet? Cut it out."

"Well, that's Art's biblical belief," said Cam. And much to my amazement he propped his pillow against the wall and leaned on it. It looked as if the guy was going to settle down and rap some...what? genealogy? world history? religion? with his little brother.

"Of course what race or religion someone is, or participates in, doesn't make the slightest bit of difference, really," he went on. "How's that saying go? 'Going to church doesn't make you a Christian any more than going to a garage makes you a car'? I like that. Don't forget that I'm the person who believes we—all of us—are One. We—all of us—no matter where we go, or don't go, to worship are Christian, Jewish, Muslim, Buddhist, animist, and atheist. Or whatever. Just as all of us are white, black, red, and yellow. We are wolf and otter, cow and whale, emerald and zircon, lima beans and eggplant, the mountains and the prairies and the deep blue sea. And all of us are also God, of course—a part of God. Everything in nature is."

He smiled at me disarmingly and gestured with one hand, palm up, as if to say "What could be simpler?" Or something. Es-

172

caping off that hilltop was probably the furthest thing from his mind just then. That left me feeling very much like lima beans or eggplant myself—a helpless vegetable, in other words.

"Art may not fully comprehend all that at the moment," he continued. "And because he's convinced he's a Christian Israelite, it's easy for him to imagine he's being illegally oppressed by the new Assyrians—the government, which has the power today that the old Assyrians had in the old days. His racist paranoia is unfortunate. But put that to one side, and you find a religious man. He wants to have God in the schoolhouse and God in the statehouse—so he's interested in partnerships with God, just as I said, and just as I am. And he similarly sees us humans as being in a partnership with nature, which he believes that God created for man's uses and enjoyment. Now, *his* partnership with nature is tilted a little more in man's favor than mine is, but I believe that if we talk about that more...."

I sat there blinking, trying to collect my thoughts. Arguing with Cam about Art was obviously hopeless. He couldn't or wouldn't focus—except fleetingly—on the negatives: that Art just wrapped himself in weird misinterpretations of history and the Bible and the U.S. Constitution to justify his own hatreds.

Cam was interested in finding similarities between himself and the Sons instead of noticing their differences. But when you came right down to it, the only thing my brother and Art Honeycutt totally agreed on was that they both wanted to be left alone.

So here we were, sitting on this hilltop. And Cam didn't want to do what *I* wanted to do, which was get off it.

So...what? It seemed wrong, in a way, to even think of try-

173

ing to *force* him to leave; he'd probably been happier here than he'd been anywhere in quite a long time.

But I didn't have his reasons for staying, any of them. Should I consider collecting Millie and making a run for the bottom of the hill? We could explain to the authorities that two innocent people were still up there, etc., etc. Maybe we could help to keep things peaceful.

The only trouble with that idea was that it involved abandoning my brother. "Only trouble with"? Try "unthinkable part of."

Just then there was the sound of footsteps in the hall outside our door. Somebody went downstairs.

Cam stroked his chin. "I should probably tell Art what I saw last night," he said slowly.

More footsteps passed by our door. It now seemed as if the entire household was up.

"He'll notice, won't he?" I asked. "As soon as he looks out the window? I mean, it's light outside." I didn't want him and Art to get into it about the guns.

Cam nodded, thinking that over—and then held up a finger.

"Hold on a minute," he said. "I'd like to see if I can get me a little advice." And with that he closed his eyes, pulled his feet up onto the bed, crossed his legs in what I think is called the lotus position, and started humming to himself—just one monotonous note, repeated again and again.

I didn't move or speak, just watched him. Time passed, quite a lot of time—at least ten minutes. I was conscious of some comings and goings downstairs, but I couldn't make out what anyone was saying.

Finally Cam's eyes snapped open. "The best-laid plans of

174

mice and men," he whispered mysteriously. And then (I think I have this right), "*La illaha illah-lah.*"

He'd barely finished saying that when an amplified voice— Art Honeycutt's—boomed out from right below our room.

"Sheriff Mays"—Art had that bullhorn out again—"your people are, as of this moment, trespassers. They're on my property illegally, and I'm asking all of you to leave. Asking *nicely*, at this point in time. And I hope that any members of the media who may be down there with you will inform their listeners and readers that I and the other men up here are all plain, God-fearing American patriots, asking nothing more from their oppressors than to be left alone."

There was no answer right away. Then this:

"Mr. Honeycutt!" The people down below had audio equipment, too—even better stuff than what Art had. "This property has been foreclosed for nonpayment of taxes. It don't belong to you no more. The new owners want to take possession. We want to do this nicely, but you have no right to remain on this land. I hereby order you to vacate these premises at once, taking only your personal possessions with you."

This time an answer came at once.

"Forget about it, Sheriff," Art replied. "Nobody's leaving, 'cept for you and all them stormtroopers of yours. An' you should know we got four visitors up here, two of which are females. They're from out of state. You can see one of their cars right close to where you are." He paused. "So now I'm *telling* you—and your men, too—to leave my property. Like I'm sure the educated media people will tell you, there ain't no taxation allowed in this country without representation, and we ain't represented anywhere! That makes your government illegal, and it's why I haven't paid no taxes. I'm giving you five minutes to move your asses out of here. After that, we're going to start shooting. And if you're tempted to shoot back, well, then we'll begin...let's call it *wounding* these visitors we got. That doesn't have to happen, though. It'll be totally up to you."

I looked at Cam—with my eyes bugging out, I'm sure. Was I alarmed by what I'd heard? Is nicotine addictive?

"Oh, and just in case you think I'm kidding you about the hostages, you keep your eyes on our front door up here." These were Art's last words. The "*hostages*"?

We left the room together, Cam and I. But before we were halfway down the stairs, we saw that Art was certainly not kidding.

They'd handcuffed Millie and Michelle together, and then they'd thrown a chain around the space between the cuffs and attached its ends to this big round cast-iron patio umbrella base. That made it function like the heavy iron ball in one of those ball-and-chain rigs they used to put on road-crew convicts. Wherever the girls went, they'd have to go together, and dragging or carrying this heavy, bulky item along with them. For now, Jesse Brink was standing in the living room holding on to it, while Sandy and Fred pushed Meesh and Millie into the open doorway.

Art was sitting in his lookout spot with some sort of rifle in his hands and the bullhorn and a pair of binoculars on the floor beside him.

After a few seconds, he nodded at Jesse and said, "Reel 'em back in." Jess gave the umbrella base a yank, and the girls were jerked back into the room. Sandy slammed the door behind them.

Cam and I just stood there, frozen. This time I really tried to think what I should do, and I didn't come up with a damn thing. Art was looking at his watch. Less than a minute (I'm guessing) later, he stepped back, aimed that gun of his out the open window, and fired it three times. The noise of that, inside the room, was just like they always say: *deafening*.

Art picked up the binoculars, looked through them, and I saw (more than heard) him chuckle.

"Look at them skedaddle!" he announced to all of us. And sorry to say, I did hear *that*, all right.

chapter 26

When Art turned away from the window, he still had a small self-satisfied smile on his face. And seeing Cam and me looking (I imagine) like a pair of freaked-out statues, halfway down the stairs, seemed to make him even happier.

"Well, hell—the gang's all here!" he bayed. He pointed with the barrel of his gun. "Suppose you boys just take yourselves a seat right there at the table. On that far bench, okay?"

We did as we were told, moving crabwise into place, me first, then Cam. I noticed Fred and Sandy also cradled rifles in their hands and arms and had them pointed, in an offhand sort of way, at us. Sandy had a blue bandanna tied around his neck, cowboy style. The expression on his face as he observed me make my way across the room shook me up a little. It wasn't gratitude, not anymore—far from it.

As we sat down on the bench, I snuck a peek at Cam. He looked both pale and outraged, possibly a little bit in shock.

"And you girls park it on the other bench," said Art. He watched them maneuver awkwardly over to the table, dragging that heavy umbrella base, and then get turned around so they could sit tight close together, facing him, with their handcuffed hands resting on their thighs.

"Lucky the two of you are sisters," Art went on, "seein' as you're going to be so close."

"But you don't need to fret," Fred Slocum blurted out. "That was just Art talking. We're not the type to do no harm to ladies." His cap was still a little off-center, and he looked stiff-necked and uncomfortable. He pulled the chair from the head of the table and sat down on it, sitting straight, not leaning back. Sandy pulled out his chair from the foot and flopped into it; you could believe that he'd do harm to *anyone*. Jesse Brink made a trip to the gun cabinet to get himself a rifle, too, and then leaned up against one of the wooden columns that supported the ceiling.

"So here we are," said Art. "What we knew was bound to happen now is taking place, just a little sooner than we figured." He pinched the tip of his nose. "Too bad the rest of the Sons ain't here—I'd like it if the sheriff knew we had, say, twenty guys up here instead of just us four. More for appearances than anything."

"Hell, who's to say they don't think we got *fifty* guys up here?" said Sandy. "We could, for all they know." His voice was still a little off.

Art pursed his lips and shook his head. "I suspect they been observing who went in and out of here awhile. I suspect he's got a pretty good idea—Sheriff Bobby Mays does." But then he brightened. "Not that it makes a hell of a lot of difference. I don't believe there's going to be much shooting either way."

"On accounta what you said about the hostages…?" said Jesse.

"Well, *that*," said Art. "But even more them wanting to avoid a Ruby Ridge–type situation. If they picked somebody off up

179

here, what that'd do is cause a whole shitload of guys to see what we been saying all along is *right*. That government *is* trampling on people's rights, even to the point of *killing* them when they stand up and try to make a point. No—a shooting is about the last thing that those guys out there are looking for."

"That kinda is too bad, you know?" said Sandy Prime.

"What—you volunteerin' to get shot?" asked Jesse. It seemed as if the older Sons were much less interested in any sort of…escalation.

"Me? Not quite," said Sandy. He laughed. "And anyway, you make a better target, man. No." He got up, walked over to the window, and pointed his rifle through it down the hill. It had a scope on it, I noticed. "I was just thinkin' if we got to shootin' back and forth, Deputy Lawrence Chisholm could be out there somewhere. An' I'd enjoy the chance to put one in the middle of that so-and-so's tin star. Ka-*pow!*" He straightened up and walked back to his chair. "I've owed ol' laughing Larry since the two of us was kids."

"And I'll bet there's some down there owe *you*," Fred muttered.

"Never mind all that," said Art. "Jesus! Pay attention to what's really going down. You *know* those gentlemen we just got rid of didn't head on home to have a second cup of coffee and turn on the *Today* show."

"But they ain't lookin' to get shot at neither," Jesse said.

"'Course not," Art replied. "And they know that they don't have to have that happen. They're going to want to talk, *negotiate*. Same as we do, boys. I bet you fifty bucks we get a phone call 'fore it's lunchtime."

And so we waited, sitting there, Fred still straight up and

Sandy tipped back in his chair. Jesse kept on standing with his back against the post.

Time started to crawl by.

"Are you okay?" I said to the women's backs after a while.

Mil turned her head and forced a little smile in my direction. "Sure," she said. "We're fine."

She looked at her sister right after she said that. I think she wanted Michelle to look at her and agree that they were fine. But Meesh's head didn't move. Her back was rounded and her head was partway down; if her eyes were open—I couldn't tell from where I was—she was staring at a point on the floor halfway between where she was and Art's stool. I looked over at Cam next. He didn't look at me, and I could tell that he was thinking, concentrating hard. He kept pursing his lips and nodding his head ever so slightly, up and down. I'd seen him do that hundreds of times when he was trying to focus on a problem and work out a solution in his head.

After a few minutes, he said, "Art?"

"What?" said Art Honeycutt without turning away from the window.

"This isn't a good idea," my brother said.

"What isn't?" said Art.

"Your calling us hostages and threatening to harm the girls. Those aren't righteous acts," said Cam.

"Well, we ain't the Righteous Brothers," Sandy Prime put in. "In case you didn't notice."

Cam ignored him. "God would not approve," he said, still looking at Art.

"We'll see," said Art. "Way I see it, if we get that call, that means God's okay with what we're doin'."

181

"You're setting yourself up for a big fall, acting this way," Cam told him. "I want you to unchain those women at once."

"You want me to," said Art, "and I don't want to. So it's up to God to break the tie. We'll just sit here and see what He decides."

Cam sucked in his breath and made a little irritated sound, but apparently he couldn't think of an answer, because he didn't say anything else.

Maybe fifteen minutes later, Meesh said, "I have to go to the bathroom," still looking at the floor.

"You can use the one upstairs," said Art. "Jesse, you go with them. And see they keep the door open. After five minutes, bring 'em out whether they're done or not."

The girls picked up that umbrella base and lugged it up the stairs, Jesse following. Beside me, Cam was shaking his head in disapproval. And as I watched them go, I started talking.

"Look," I said to Art. "You really don't need four hostages...."

At that point I started thinking in addition to talking. What was I saying? Did I think I was in a movie? Was I about to make some grand heroic gesture, volunteering to be the sole hostage if they let the others go? Was I willing to be at the mercy of Sandy Prime up here with no one except the other Sons to witness whatever he might decide to do to me?

Jesus, Chris, I thought.

"Or *any* hostages, really," came out of my mouth next. I was thinking, Well, the girls hadn't heard what I'd started to say and who knows if it had even registered on Cam. And anyway, no one could possibly know what it was I almost said. "You could come across to the sheriff as a really decent and humane and reasonable guy..." I added.

Sandy Prime started laughing then, even before Art Honeycutt said, "Forget it, sonny."

I shut up. My heart was pounding and I felt humiliated. Maybe I *should* have volunteered to stay if he let my brother and Millie—and Meesh, of course—go. But I hadn't been able to do that. I'd started to, but then I'd chickened out like the perfect little Craven that I was. How could I claim to love either Cam or Millie if I wasn't willing to put myself in a little greater danger for their sakes?

I think it was then that the nightmare quality of this whole scene really hit me. Here I was, sitting next to my brother, whom I'd set out to "save" a couple of weeks—was it?—before. Me—totally ignorant about mental illness and wanting to avoid getting a summer job—actually expecting I'd find Cam and bring him home because...because...well, because I *wanted* to, and I was a spoiled middle-class kid who was pretty much used to getting what he wanted.

If I hadn't had such a crazy idea in the first place, I'd never have met Meesh and I wouldn't be here now, and neither would she and Millie, probably, because lacking money, they'd have had to hitch rides (if they decided to take the trip at all), and that would have taken them a whole lot longer. And if *we* weren't here, Cam wouldn't be in the fix he was in now—the actual physical fix or the mental turmoil he must be going through as a result of everything our being here had forced him to find out. Some *frater* I'd turned out to be.

But then I told myself I absolutely shouldn't think that way. I might have been naive, but my motives had been okay. I'd been *trying*, for Cam's sake. And all wasn't lost. Art didn't want a shoot-out. There'd be a settlement of some sort. I could still bring my brother home. I put my hand on his knee and squeezed. I wanted him to feel how much I loved him. The girls and Jesse came back downstairs while I was doing that.

"Now, if they call"—Fred Slocum broke the silence this time—"we'll negotiate with them on the phone?"

"Hell, no," said Art. "What'd be the point of that? Nobody'd *hear*, except the one guy I was talking to. We want to get the message out. Which means we don't say anything at any time unless the whole world's listening—and taking notes. It's really sorta funny. The media, which is mostly owned by Jews and foreigners, turns out to be the best friend that we got! We're looking at coverage here that'd cost us more than a million dollars, I bet, if we had to pay for it in adver*t*isements."

"So when they call us up—*if* they do—what we say is *what*?" asked Jesse.

"We say that some of them can come up to the gate, unarmed and with their bullhorn, and we'll talk," said Art. "*Provided* that reporters from the TV, magazines, and papers all are present. We'll tell them cameras and tape recorders are *required*, man."

"You thinking that they'll put you on TV?" asked Fred.

"Yeah, bein' led away in cuffs and shackles, more'n likely," said Sandy with a wink.

"Shoot," said Art. "That ain't gonna happen either. Even if we do surrender sometime, they couldn't do too much to us. It ain't like we *killed* anybody or blew up any pretty little office buildings. And hell, after we get done, I bet we get donations that'll cover our expenses here. There's plenty of good Americans out there that's bound to help us once they know what we're about."

"However," Sandy said, "it could be days and days before all this plays out. What're we going to do with these four in the meantime?" He waggled his gun in our direction.

"I've thought on that," Art told him. "The main ones we need are the girls. People care about women and children getting hurt or killed much more'n guys. And probably we'll have to let them see the girls again in a couple of days—no way do we settle fast. We want to drag this out, keep it in the news for even weeks. But most of the time, let's keep 'em in the bunkhouse. We can chain them to one of the woodstoves in there. Those sonsabitches are *heavy*; no way they could ever budge 'em. Nighttimes, one of us can stay down there with them."

Of course I had to look at Sandy Prime when Art said that. And to my horror Sandy'd turned his head and was already looking at *me*. And then without making any big deal of it, he winked and licked his lips.

"And how about them other two?" said Fred.

"I don't think it makes a hell of a lot of difference what we do with them," said Art. "At some point maybe we'd be smart to let 'em go—'release' them, like they always say on the news, with hostages. The big one eats too much, and we got no use for loony Cam no more."

"You rotten lying *fraud*!" Cam leaped to his feet as he said— no, shouted—that, and slid out from between the bench and the table before I even thought to try and grab him.

I don't know what he was planning on doing, and his anger never had turned violent before, but he was heading for Art Honeycutt. He surely never even saw Jesse Brink's big fist coming at his head. But as soon as it hit him—with an ugly *thunk*— he turned into a rag doll, going over sideways fast, then crumpled on the floor, not moving.

185

Meesh (I guess it was) let out a little cry. I got up and headed for him. Nobody tried to stop me. It probably was pretty obvious that all I had in mind was trying to help my fallen brother.

I'd never seen a person punched like that before. And Jesse'd done it almost casually, as if he were swatting a fly. "Sucker-punched," it's called—when the person who gets hit is not expecting to be hit and doesn't have a chance to block the blow or go with it or brace himself or *anything*. It's about the worst way to get hit there is, I think.

I knelt beside my brother, reluctant at the very first to touch him. It was possible he had a broken neck, I thought; he even *could* be dead; he surely was unconscious. Then I saw that he was breathing, and his head wasn't at any weird angle away from his neck. So I sort of straightened him out a little on his back. One side of his face was red and swelling up already. It occurred to me that maybe a cold wet dishtowel would feel good to him and maybe even help him come to. I got up and went over by the kitchen sink and got one.

As I was doing that the telephone rang and Art answered it. This was the call he'd been expecting.

During the next space of time—I've no idea how long exactly; looking back, I'm guessing it must have been more than half an hour—I tried to *will* Cam back to consciousness. He seemed to be breathing normally, but his eyes didn't open, nor did he answer when I spoke his name. I put a series of cold wet towels on his forehead and pressed them gently on his poor bruised face. A couple of times I told Meesh and Millie, "He's going to be okay," though I wasn't sure if I believed that myself.

And all during that space of time I also took in, in some

186

sense of those words, all that was said and happening elsewhere in the room.

Art apparently had predicted right. The sheriff and his cohorts wanted to negotiate, and Art instructed him to come back to the gate down below in an hour, unarmed and bringing with him only "one of the feds"—plus all the members of the media.

Once that instruction had been given, Art turned to "the boys"; they had important jobs to do. First off, they were to "escort" Meesh and Millie to the bunkhouse and fasten the chain from their handcuffs to one of the heavy sheet-steel Fisher woodstoves. Then he wanted them to separate and go down the hill, each one on a different side, to make sure the sheriff was playing fair and they weren't in any danger of being snuck up on.

"Take your time," I think I heard Art say. "I want to *know* that our perimeter's secure."

Jesse asked, "We don't want to do no shooting, right?"

"Absolutely not," said Art. "You only shoot 'em if you want to *fry*. Tell you what you *can* do, though, if you see anyone. Fire in the air three times and close together. Then I'll know old Bobby Mays is trying to be clever, which of course is one thing he won't ever be. And I'll make sure that them reporters understand what's going on."

With that worked out, Fred and Sandy and Jesse unhooked the girls from the umbrella base and headed out of there with them, carrying their rifles, looking purposeful. They were feeling important, I imagine, going "on patrol." Three morons playing soldier was the way I saw it.

I tried to remember if I'd heard that an unconscious person was better off sitting up, or what. I wasn't sure, but I thought maybe Cam's head should be elevated at least, so I moved him onto a sofa and propped his head up with one of its cushions.

I think it was while I was doing that—moving Cam and trying to make him comfortable—that I decided I should get him off that hilltop, and the girls too, as soon as possible. He didn't have any future up there, and I wasn't about to let Sandy Prime be Millie's roommate in the bunkhouse.

Now *was* the time, it seemed to me. With Sandy, Jesse and Fred all gone I could...simply *do it*. All it'd take would be a simple plan, and one was in my mind already. One, two, three; simple, simple, simple—that was what I told myself. Just keep it simple, stupid—the simpler the better. I could start to do it right away, at once.

"I'm going to get a breath of air," I told Art Honeycutt, and went out through the kitchen onto the deck.

Of course he didn't mind. Why should he care what a simpleton like me was doing? He probably was thinking how his place would look—and he would sound—on national TV, the network evening news.

chapter 27

Of course I had a great deal on my mind in addition to fresh air and taking breaths of it. Once on the deck, I walked straight across it and down the four little wooden steps that led from it to the ground. Once again my destination was the bunkhouse, and this time I didn't have to be concerned about anyone seeing me go. The other three were long gone from the hilltop and Art, looking downslope through his window, couldn't see me if he tried.

Inside the bunkhouse I found Meesh and Millie sprawled on one of the lowers. Their chain went through one of the air-draft holes on the woodstove's door.

"Chris!" said Millie, sitting up. She looked glad to see me.

"How's Cam doing?" Michelle asked, eager for good news.

"I'm not sure," I think I said. "He hasn't come around, but otherwise he seems okay—his breathing and all. We're going to take him out of here. Stand up."

I knew exactly what we were going to do. I must have planned it out while I was walking over. Step one—for me to do—was pull the stovepipe away from the back of the stove. Once that was done, the stove was not connected or attached to anything—except the girls, of course. That made it (I had told

189

myself) like a very heavy barbell—probably three hundred pounds, maybe three fifty—that was also very oddly (badly) shaped.

Fisher stoves are deeper than they're wide. You put logs in end first from in front. The stove's top has two levels; it's lower in the front and slopes sharply up to the second level. That means its rear end, being bigger, is much heavier.

I told the girls to stand right near the front of the stove and when I gave the word, to squat a little and get their hands under it. Millie's right hand should be near one front leg and Meesh's left hand near the other; their handcuffed hands would grip it under the middle of the stove's front.

I went and took a similar position by the back of the stove. On the count of three, I told them, we were going to pick up the stove, keeping our backs straight and lifting with our legs. Then, I said, we were going to carry the stove out of the bunkhouse and into the barn.

We would stop and put the stove down on the way, I told them, and have a little rest. Then we would carry it to the small barn door, where we would put it down again. I would open the door and also open the back door of Michelle's Honda, which was on the main floor of the barn. We would carry the stove to the Honda, where I would set the stove's back feet on the back door's sill. Then I would join them at the front of the stove and, working together, we would somersault the stove onto the car's backseat—and they would get in after it.

I said all that in part so I could hear it being said, I think. So I could listen to my plan and see if it had any flaws. Now, I thought it sounded fine. A little hard, but fine.

"We can *lift* that?" Michelle asked, nodding at the stove.

"Yes," I said. "I'm good at lifting. Just be careful of your chain. You don't want to trip on it, and it'll be dragging along beside your feet the whole way. Ready now? Let's get our grips." I wasn't looking for any discussion at that point.

When I squatted, they did too.

"On three," I told them. "All set? One, two, three."

We lifted the thing up. It was hugely heavy, more than I'd expected, even. We staggered a little under the weight of it but then regained our balance. The rounded steel edge of the stove's underside cut into my hands—and of course the girls' hands, too—but putting it back down was not an option.

"All right, let's go," I said. I could feel them looking at me. I didn't want to meet their eyes. "We'll take it nice and easy."

The stove pulled at our shoulders. The effort we were making had us panting before we even reached the bunkhouse door. The flesh in my hands was squashed; I could feel the steel against my hand bones.

When I thought we'd gone halfway to the barn, I said, "Let's set it down."

We stood there blowing, looking at this black steel monstrosity, hating it, I'm sure. It was crazy to even think of picking it up again, but that's what we were going to do. There wasn't any choice; if it didn't go in the car, the girls didn't either; it was just that simple.

"Ready?" And I did look at them this time. Both were looking straight at me. But not pleadingly, like, "It hurts too much" and "We can't do it." They were more like "Ready!" and "Let's go!" No one *ever* tell me, please, that women aren't tough.

"Once more on the three," I said. "One, two, *three*."

And we were off again. "*Whoof-whoof-whoof!*" was what our

breathing sounded like. I could feel my pulse pounding in my head; my hands got numb this time.

We made it to the half-glass door and set the horror down again. I tried to get some feeling back into my hands as I opened that door and then the car door. It was dim inside but nowhere near as dark as the night before. We'd gotten to the tricky part.

At least it was a much shorter carry through the barn's door and to the car. When we got there, I had to twist my body and sort of drop the legs on my end of the stove onto the car door's little sill. Then I moved quickly around Millie's rear end and got *my* hands under the front of the stove on either side of their handcuffed hands.

Okay. Now a lot of the stove's weight was on its back legs, which were on the sill. And the three of us were about to execute the last step in this plan. We were going to lift up, hard, on the front end of the stove, while also pushing hard. Theoretically, we would thus be able to flip the stove over, upside down, so it'd land feet-side up on the upholstered backseat of the car. Then we'd push it as far as we could so as to make a little room for Millie and Michelle on that same seat. The front seats were reserved for Cam and me.

"Okay, this is it," I said. "One gigantic heave should do it. The chain is long enough so it won't be a problem—just let's all of us make sure we're not standing on the thing. Okay? We give this everything we've got, and then we can relax. On three again? One, two, *three!*"

I know that I, for one, let out a roar right after "three." That just seemed to go with the explosive effort, the most total, all-body effort I'd ever made in my life; I swear the muscles in my *eyelids* played a part. The stove leaped up, somersaulted, and slid, its legs up in the air. And the three of us, off-balance and still driving forward, fell in after it and collapsed in a gasping heap on the third of the car seat that the monster didn't occupy.

When I could, I straightened up and said, "Now I'll get Cam. It shouldn't take too long. Just wait right here." That last will give you an idea of the shape I was in. What *else* were they going to do?

But they both sat up and nodded. I felt like kissing them then, but this was not a time for any sort of celebration. No, not yet.

I walked back to the deck, rubbing my hands together and flexing them the whole way. My stomach muscles felt...*unsettled*, and my shoulders and my back hurt—but the plan was working so far. Once on the deck, I took a look on down the slope.

I guess Art's hour was up. Quite a crowd was outside the gate. A man wearing a gray uniform, a broad-brimmed hat, and sheriff's star stood beside another man in a jacket and tie who wore a dark blue baseball cap with some white letters on the front. Off to one side, a little ways away from them, was a small but animated pack of newspeople, perhaps a dozen of them (a lot with cameras or camcorders in hand). A few more of the same were still emerging from the trees and coming up the road behind them.

I went back into the house. Cam was sitting up! He was in that lotus position again and staring straight at Art.

"Cam!" I said, coming up to him. "Thank God. How you feeling, frat?"

He didn't answer me. He didn't turn his head or even blink.

193

"Cam, talk to me," I said. "Are you all right?" I sat down next to him.

He seemed to be breathing perfectly normally, but he wasn't responding—not to me, anyway. I leaned around so that my face was right in front of his. Not a flicker; the expression "blank stare" took on new meaning for me.

"Get that crazy asshole out of here," Art Honeycutt ordered me. "Take him outside or something. He's giving me the creeps."

Talk about a lucky break! I was being told to do the very thing I'd hoped to talk Art into. But Cam's condition bothered me. What was going on with him? From somewhere in my memory banks I pulled these two words: "catatonic seizure." I *thought* they had to do with when a mental patient gets all rigid and tunes out everyone and everything. Maybe that was from *One Flew Over the Cuckoo's Nest.*

I picked up Cam—one hand under his legs, one arm around his body, his head sort of resting on my shoulder. He still wasn't responsive in any way, but at least he didn't stay rigid, frozen in that lotus position; I was glad of that. I walked through the kitchen and out onto the deck again, heading for that little stairway to the ground.

As I reached it and started to go down, I heard Art shout through his bullhorn, "Hey! No vehicles! Back that goddamn Humvee up and outta here! How do I know it ain't full of Green Berets?"

I went down the first three steps just fine. But my next stride was too long, I guess. I landed on the edge of step four, hitting it with the very back of my heel. That caused that foot, my right one, to fly off the step when I tried to put my weight on it. My head and shoulders jerked back suddenly. I had no balance, I was helpless, falling. I landed on my right shoulder on the staircase and that hurt like hell, but at least Cam, cradled in my arms, had had his fall cushioned by my body.

And as I hit the stairs, I thought I heard a shot from somewhere. Maybe there were three shots, but just one registered.

I wasn't interested in shots, however. I was following a simple plan that, happily, was working. I started to get up.

That turned out to be a little difficult. Because I'd fallen awkwardly, I'd landed in a way that messed my shoulder up—sprained it, or whatever. It hurt, and worse than that, I soon found out it wasn't good for lifting anymore. So, using only my left arm, I started trying to move Cam around and get him draped over my one good shoulder.

That was when the miracle occurred.

"Hold on there, bro," he said quite clearly. I let him go; he straightened up and faced me. "What's going on?"

You can imagine what I felt—the sublime relief and total gratefulness. He'd come out of it, whatever it was. I had my brother back!

"We're getting out of here," I told him, speaking slowly, carefully. I didn't want to fluster him in any way. "Meesh and Millie are in your car in the barn. Now's the time for us to get away."

This was a critical moment, I realized. Would Cam agree to leave the hilltop? What if he refused and started running?

He touched the side of his head. It was swollen and multicolored, ugly-looking now. "Yes," he said. "Art is an evil spirit, maybe a false prophet, even. He deceived me." He moved his jaw a little and put his fingers to his face again. "I may have something broken here." He'd kept his voice down, too.

"Can you walk okay?" I asked him. "We really ought to move along."

He nodded. "Yes. I think so. It's just my head that hurts."

I closed my eyes and took a really deep breath. We started walking, side by side.

Meesh and Millie got excited at the sight of him. They had the right front door open, and Cam went around and got in. That was fine with me; I wanted to do the driving—see my plan through to its end. Now all I had to do was slide the barn doors open and zoom out of there.

That wasn't easy. My right side really wasn't working well, and any attempt to make it work was very painful. But using just my left arm, I got the heavy doors to—slowly, slowly—move apart. Then I reached awkwardly around and dug the car keys out of my right pants pocket. I opened the the driver's-side door and dropped my weight onto the seat, holding my bad arm in front of me. I might have made a little sound while doing that.

"Chris!" That was Millie; I recognized her voice. "You're bleeding. It looks like you've been shot!"

I didn't answer. I turned the key with my left hand and the car started; I shoved the thing into gear. It was an automatic and that made everything easier. I did not believe what Millie said— how could she know what being shot looked like? I'd hurt my shoulder falling on it while carrying a hundred-seventy-pound dead weight. I'd probably sprained the damn thing and scraped it on the edge of that stair. Kids like me did not get shot. Mil was…dramatizing.

I suppose I braked just before I got to the gate, but I hit it pretty hard and it popped open. The sheriff and the guy in civvies and the media people had seen me coming, of course, and had gotten out of

196

the way, but as soon as we stopped, they rushed toward us. Meesh or Millie'd rolled down the right back window, and one of them was shouting that someone should call an ambulance. I thought that sounded like a good idea: Cam wasn't in any condition to deal with the authorities, much less the media, and he did need medical attention. I decided to remain inside the car for the time being. I didn't feel like being jostled by the crowd that had surrounded us. If I didn't move at all, my shoulder didn't hurt that bad.

From up above Art Honeycutt was hollering. "What the *hell* is going on? My car's been stolen!" And then, "Sandy! Jesse! Fred! Get back here, quick!" Followed by, "Listen, Mays— you're breaking our agreement. Whoever stole my goddamn car—you better have arrested him!"

By then I had the sheriff and his sidekick right beside me, asking questions through the window.

I put up my left hand to try to slow them down.

"Look," I said, "my brother here's been hurt. And our friends in the backseat are handcuffed together and chained to that stove. We need an ambulance and somebody with a hacksaw or bolt cutters or something who can cut them free—all right? Could you get us some help right away? I'm not feeling too hot myself—we've been held up there for a couple of days, and that's our story in a nutshell. There's four of them, I guess you know that: Honeycutt and Sandy Prime and Fred somebody and a big guy named Jesse." I couldn't find their last names in my mind just then.

I guess I was pretty spacey at that point. I looked over at Cam. His window was rolled up and I think he'd locked the door. He'd closed his eyes, and I thought he might be—how had he put it?—trying to "get a little advice."

197

What mattered was that he was alive and that I'd actually found him, and that it looked as if he might come home with me, although that bridge was still a ways ahead of us. But I'd done what I'd set out to do, something I'd stupidly believed (it seemed like an age ago) would be quite easy.

By then a lot of county cars and pickups and police cruisers—and yes, a Humvee even—had come steaming up the road. Some of them stopped quite near us, while others kept on following Art's fence, in both directions. Someone arrived with a cutting tool and freed Michelle and Millie, and Mil came around to my side of the car and told me a rescue squad ambulance was parked out on the county highway, and it'd be along any minute. She said that everything would soon be "hunky-dory." It stuck in my mind, her saying that. Just about then I'd started thinking that perhaps I *had* been shot.

"We've explained to them about Cam being hit and how he'd been in shock or something for a while," she said next. "But they'd like to ask you a few more things if you can stand it—just while we're waiting for the ambulance. I told them I thought you'd been shot."

"Sure," I said. "I guess I can talk all right. Just so I don't have to move."

So I answered a bunch of questions put to me by the guy in civvies (FBI was on his cap) and the sheriff, and when it seemed they were about done, some other uniforms appeared with none other than Sandy Prime in tow. But now he was the one who had the handcuffs on, and he looked as if he might have had rough handling.

"Here's the guy who fired the shot from the trees back there," one of the troopers told the sheriff. He used his thumb to indicate where "back there" was—behind where all of them were now, back in the trees, farther from the compound. Sandy must have come down the back of the hill and then, just on his own, decided to cross the mowed area, get under cover, and circle back around to the front.

"Must be he had some score to settle with the Sons or something," one trooper said.

"Not damn likely," said the sheriff. "He's one of them. That's Sandy Prime."

"He was aiming at me," I said. Now I knew it. I *had* been shot, just as Millie'd said—by Sandy Prime himself. He'd hit me on the shoulder, but if I hadn't slipped on those steps—who knows?—he might have killed me.

"He wanted to get even," I said. "For something that happened up there."

"Hell, I bet he had more than getting even on his mind," the FBI guy said. "He was trying to set us up, make it look like the authorities were picking people off again—one of the hostages this time. He wanted this to be another Ruby Ridge, I bet."

"Goddamn it, Mays, you all are trespassing!" Art screamed from up the hill. But he sounded different than he had when we were there with him—not so confident, so much in charge this time.

The ambulance arrived, and Cam and I got loaded into it. Millie said that she and Meesh would follow in the car, driven by a trooper.

chapter 28

I'm a little fuzzy about the next few hours. The ride in the ambulance seemed pretty long at the time, and later on I found out it truly was: The hospital was more than fifty miles away.

There were two rescue squad people to take care of us, a guy who doubled as the driver and a woman who sat in the back with Cam and me during the whole trip. As soon as we were on board, they checked our vital signs and got a bandage on me. The good news, they said, was that the bullet hadn't hit an artery, so the bleeding wasn't all that bad. When we got under way, they radioed ahead for someone to meet us along the way who was trained to do things they weren't allowed to, like administer painkillers.

Both of the rescue squadders were really nice, and the lady in the back seemed impressed by what she'd been told about "the escape," and the part I'd played in it.

Typically, my brother had to gild that lily, telling her I'd always been outstanding all my life.

"He's a brother in a million," he insisted. "Really smart— and *good*. He drove all the way out here to see me, and once he got the girls in the car, he came back and carried me out of Art's house when I was, like, completely out of it, I guess. He got me away from a very bad situation back there."

Obviously Meesh must have filled him in about what happened when he wasn't...functioning.

"Yes, I heard that," the woman said.

So then Cam asked her some questions about the Sons— how many of them there were, all told, and how they were perceived by people who live in the area.

"I don't believe there's that many of them," the woman told him. "Maybe twenty or thirty is all—and some of those not real committed. A lot of folks around here have trouble paying their taxes, but most everybody sees the need for them. There's no reason Art Honeycutt should be any different—that's the way I look at it. The ones that joined up with him aren't exactly the cream of the county, I can tell you that much."

My brother went along with that.

"They were—they are—dishonest. They lied to me repeatedly," he said. "I'm not sure they have any real beliefs other than that they should be allowed to do whatever they feel like."

"That seems about right," she agreed.

"It so happens I believe there are a lot of things wrong with the way things work nowadays, too," Cam told her. Maybe it was relief—a reaction to all he'd been through, coming out of shock and everything—but something certainly had pushed his play button.

"I think people do need to get back to basics," he went on, "to rediscover the strength of their own senses, for instance. Most of us have the capacity to see and hear and taste and smell and *feel* more keenly than we do. We've become much too dependent on our cars, TV's, and processed, instant foods. We overgraze, and overfish, and pollute and otherwise destroy the natural world. We rely on government, not God. And where has all this gotten us?"

"I really wouldn't know," the woman said after a short pause in which she looked over at me.

"My cheek hurts," Cam said. "Or my jaw, I guess it is. I'm worried something may be broken in there."

"You probably ought to try not to move your jaw too much," the woman said, "until they take a look at the hospital."

"That's good advice," my brother said. "I'll just shut up and take it easy, the way Chris is doing. Are you all right there, bro? Don't fight the pain. If you relax and sort of go with it, you'll help your body heal itself, you know."

I gave a grunt of what I intended to be agreement, and Cam said, "Good—and so I *will* shut up, right now. But if you need something, you say so—all right? A drink or anything. This lady's here to help you."

I made another grunt and he said, "I'm going to start *my* healing process, too." And then he actually did shut up.

At the hospital I was x-rayed, then taken right to the OR, where the bullet was removed and the wound cleaned out. That's all hearsay, of course; I don't remember any of it. Afterward I was pretty groggy, and I believe I had a little conversation with a nurse. But when I came back to full consciousness, I was in a bed in a private room, nicely bandaged, and Millie was in a chair right next to me. She told me the doctor said the bullet had been stopped by the top of my humerus, which is the big bone that runs from the elbow to the shoulder. They'd given me more stuff for pain, of course, and a ton of antibiotics, she said, but they wanted me to stick around for a few days so they could be sure no infection had set in. Apparently—and unfortunately—they believed the shoulder would probably need some further repair when I got home.

I asked how Cam was doing and she said he had a broken jaw but otherwise was fine. He was currently asleep, she said, watched over by Meesh. Luckily his break was a kind that didn't even call for the jaw to be wired shut.

"Cam just nodded when they told him that," Millie said to me. "As if he wasn't at all surprised. And then he said, 'Just wait until you see how fast it heals. You'll be amazed.'"

"I bet they will be, too," I said without even thinking. And after I said it, I realized that in spite of everything, I still believed—or believed *in*—Cam. That didn't mean I'd swallow whole, or agree with, everything he said or thought. It was more that I still believed he was—as everyone likes to say about people—"special," in lots of different ways, some positive and some a bit (a lot?) delusional. I guess I liked thinking that though he needed help, he also could be a real help, too. I liked to think I still had things to learn from him.

Then suddenly I thought of something—someone—else, another member of the family.

"My God, I've got to call my mother," I told Mil. "I promised her I would as soon as I found Cam. I just hope we didn't get a mention on some news report. I think the sheriff wrote our names down."

Millie went and got a telephone that she could plug in by my bed.

It was past bedtime back home, and my mother answered on the second ring. I geared myself up for a really big effort.

"Hi, Mom. It's me, Chris," I began. Not too original an opening.

"Chris, I swear…" And off she went—the hour didn't matter. *Responsibility* and *consideration* were her themes—subjects that she'd touched on once or twice before with me.

I tried to interrupt, but my halfhearted attempt was no match for her passion.

"So where are you exactly?" she concluded. "Is Cam actually *there?*"

"He is," I said. "I found him." And I must admit I put a note of triumph in my voice. "We're both in a hospital, but we're both fine. I was shot, and he has a broken jaw, I guess."

That cooled her jets, as the saying goes, and her flabbergastedness (if that's a word) gave me the opportunity to babble out a very much condensed description of the Sons of Liberty Two and Cam's involvement with them, and how it had ended violently.

"But we managed to escape," I concluded, "after they got the place surrounded. It was just like on TV, with one of those militias, or that Republic of Texas outfit." I was trying to sound like my normal self.

My mother finally found her voice again.

"And you were *shot* by someone? And Cam had his jaw broken? Are you sure you're both all right? Should I come out there? I'm having trouble taking all this *in*," she said. "As you recall, I'm sure, I never was crazy about your going off looking for Cam. But I hardly thought you'd get yourself involved in something like *this*. Is there a doctor or someone I could speak to? And can Cam *talk?* When can you come home, do you know? He *will* come with you, won't he?"

I guess it was natural that my mother wanted to speak to a fellow adult, rather than (or in addition to) me, her teenage son. I told her it might be easier if I got the doctor to call *her*, but she insisted I give her the name of the hospital and its address. But before we hung up, I was able to tell her how Cam seemed to be and urge her not to have him taken into some kind of mental-health custody. I also assured her there was no reason whatsoever for her to come way out here.

"There isn't any place Cam wants to run away to now," I told her. "And I believe he trusts me and that woman I came out here with—Michelle, the one from Gramercy Manor. Once we get an okay from the doctor, I'm pretty sure we'll be able to head home on our own, no sweat."

"Well, we'll see," my mother said. "I must say you don't *sound* like someone who's been shot." Her voice had suddenly gotten softer and more Mom-like. "And Chris—I'm so relieved that Cam is there with you and this Michelle woman. I guess it may have been a good thing you went looking for him, honey, after all. With him having been hurt and everything. It's just been so much for me to take in, as I said. I mean, I never did *expect....*"

So before we hung up, we managed to achieve a degree of normalcy (I guess you'd call it)—and for me a degree of exhaustion from the effort I'd just made. I knew she'd call the hospital—and Cam at some point—and check up on the "facts" I'd given her, but that was fine with me. And even if it wasn't, there was no way I could stop her. It's a free country, no matter what Art Honeycutt may think.

I asked Millie if she thought it was possible for me to get something to eat. It seemed that talking to my mother hadn't only tired me—it had also revived my appetite.

* * *

We stayed in the area for another ten days, Cam and I in the hospital and the sisters in a motel. My mother didn't join us. Cam's face and jaw didn't require much medical attention, but he liked the peacefulness of the hospital, and the doctors, realizing he was a kind of special case (and not needing his bed for other patients), decided they'd just let him stay. I asked our doc about getting a psychiatrist to prescribe some medication for Cam, maybe just as a preventative, but he told me he was sure no colleague would do that without taking the time to learn a great deal more about the person being prescribed for—and that would involve an amount of time we weren't planning to spend at this location. That made sense to me, and inasmuch as Cam wasn't hearing, or saying, or doing anything out of the ordinary, it seemed his "treatment" could be put on hold a little while.

After some discussion, we decided to drive home, taking both cars, sticking close to one another, eating meals together, and sleeping in motels at night. Millie and Meesh drove the automatic (the car she'd loaned to Cam), and Cam and I rode in mine, which was a stick.

Cam drove almost the whole way. I *could* drive, but holding the steering wheel made my shoulder ache, and when I took a pain pill, I got sleepy. Cam is a good driver and I wasn't at all fearful that he'd do something peculiar or dangerous. I'd asked our doctor what he thought, and he agreed with me. Cam's problems had never affected his vision or coordination—and he had driven all the way out there alone without any trouble. Also, Cam knew I *needed* him to do this, which gave him extra reasons to be careful and controlled.

I was a little more concerned about the girls, to tell you the truth. Ever since they'd adjusted Meesh's medication she'd been fine, but Millie'd said her sister hadn't been the best of drivers, ever. So it was agreed ahead of time that if ever Meesh felt the least bit sleepy, she'd let Millie drive. Mil didn't have a license or a whole lot of experience, but during the time we were in the hospital she and Meesh went driving every day, and she felt fully capable of filling in as needed.

That was a little irresponsible, I guess—our deciding to do things that way—but it all worked out. Mil hardly drove at all, and each night we'd take adjoining rooms at whatever motel we chose, one ostensibly for the guys and the other for the girls, though that wasn't how we ended up.

I loved sleeping with Millie—by which I mean being in the same bed with her. My shoulder didn't permit any writhing around, but we could kiss and touch a little and just generally rejoice at being with each other. I have no idea what Cam and Meesh did next door, but whatever it was agreed with them. Whenever they were together they were sweet and loving, not in a sappy way, but more as if there was a bond between them that they both treasured. That had been true, I realized, from the moment on that hike of ours when Cam had kissed her hand.

chapter 29

I called my mother every night, en route, and Cam talked to her as well. We thought these calls might lessen the awkwardness of our arrival, wounded, and with two strange (to Mom) young women who were, in fact, our girlfriends—and who we'd asked to stay in her house "awhile."

I'd apprised her of Millie's existence before we left the hospital, and her initial reaction had been not so hot. How come I hadn't mentioned this girl before? she wanted to know. Was I ashamed of her? Why had she "tagged along," anyway? It was once again as if she thought there was some plot afoot to take advantage of my gullibility or inexperience. I was thinking whether I liked it or not, she'd always see me as her baby.

"Wait. I don't get what you're implying, Mom," I finally said to her. "You mean, these two evil sisters were hoping I'd get her pregnant so I'd have to marry her? Or maybe it'll turn out she's fifteen and they can threaten to charge me with statutory rape unless I pay them a small fortune in hush money?"

She said of course that wasn't it, but that it just seemed peculiar to her that someone in the mental-health field would drag along a younger sister on a search for a man she knew had "certain problems."

Telling my mother that Meesh was not some kind of therapist but had been a fellow patient of Cam's at Gramercy Manor was a thing we decided to put off until later—just one of several things, in fact. I figured at some point shortly after our arrival I could explain to her that I myself hadn't known for a long time what Michelle's exact status was—which was perfectly true. I also figured that once Mom had seen for herself how sweet and good for Cam Meesh was (and, hopefully, how "normal"), she'd handle the truth a little better.

Our actual arrival went very well. It turned out that Mom had done something really smart: She'd gotten her sister, my aunt Margaret, to come down for a visit. She's a large and cheerful person, a king-size bundle of energy, and she helped Mom out with the preparations for our invasion, and then the care and feeding of us four. Best of all, she kept things light with her "Isn't that just wonderful?" approach to…everything.

The four of us had done a lot of conferring in the course of our trip and had come up with what we called our master plan. Its centerpiece was that after a few significant days at our house, Meesh and Millie would go home, where they would pack up in preparation for moving down near us! The idea was that before they left, we'd find them an apartment—Cam and I would go in on the rent—and later Meesh would get a job and Mil would go to school with me. Long term, Michelle wanted to be a physical therapist—she'd had two years of college—but she'd decided to put the training part of the plan on hold until Cam's situation got worked out. Meesh and Millie were convinced their father wouldn't raise objections, and that, in fact, he'd love to see his younger daughter living with her sister, thus relieving him of all responsibility for her. Mr. Falk, both believed, was more than ready to stop parenting.

Cam's "situation" (or whatever you want to call it) had been the thing that weighed on me the most as we started heading home. Pretty soon his jaw would be completely healed, his doctor'd said. And it *seemed* as if he hadn't suffered any ill effects from all the other stuff that happened at Art Honeycutt's that last day—being called loony and learning that he'd been used by people who he'd thought respected him and his ideas.

But what did that mean, if anything? I had no idea if he still thought he was getting messages from God, for instance, or if he still believed all that weird stuff he'd told Lisa. There wasn't any obvious reason why he suddenly wouldn't. So how would he feel about getting together with some representatives of the mental-health establishment when we got back home?

I wondered if I ought to talk to Michelle and ask her what *she* thought—or maybe ask her to ask Cam and then tell me what he said.

But I decided it wouldn't be the proper thing to do. This was up to me, just the way getting him off that hilltop had been up to me. I was his brother, after all—the only one he'd ever have. I'd just have to pretend that I was Cam and he was Chris.

So on the day before we arrived home, when we stopped for lunch at one of those enormous truck stops just off the interstate, I asked Cam to stay put in the car for a few minutes before we went in—that there was something I wanted to talk with him about. Meesh and Millie had pulled into the next parking space, and I rolled down the window, told them to grab a table, and we'd join them in a little bit. They both gave me puzzled looks, but at least they didn't put them into words.

"Here's what I want to talk about," I said to Cam. "When we get home..."

He'd turned in my direction and was looking at me with his head slightly bowed, through the tops of his eyes, and with a little smile in place. He'd put up a hand to stop me.

"First let me ask you something, Chris," he said. "How do you think I am right now? In terms of my...stability, I mean. Just tell me the truth."

"That's related to what I wanted to ask *you*," I said. "As far as I can tell, you're doing great—just fine." It wasn't that surprising that he'd (kind of) read my mind. He'd been doing that for years. I was ready to go on, but once again he stopped me.

"You think I'm 'fine'?" he said. "Is that your diagnosis? That there's nothing the matter with ol' Cam? You think I'm *normal*, Chris? Art Honeycutt sure didn't." He gave a little laugh.

He was making this easy for me, I thought. In a way. He'd raised the subject of his mental health. But what I wanted was for *him* to tell *me* how he was.

"Art Honeycutt is full of it," I said. "You're about the most intelligent and thoughtful person I've ever known. Of course you aren't anything like 'crazy.' You don't rant and rave and think you're George Washington or Elvis."

Cam smiled at that. "No, luckily I don't," he said. "But I've been thinking about...about some of the experiences I've thought I had, and Michelle and I've been talking about them, too, at night. You know how I believed—and she did, too—that God was speaking to me? I'm not so sure about that now. Maybe that was something I imagined...something, I don't know, like wishful

211

thinking or something. It hasn't happened since you got me down from Art's." He shook his head. "The truth is, I don't know what's going on with me. Like Meesh says, there are so many things I want so much—for me personally and for the whole society..."

"What I want to know," I said, "before we get home, is whether you'd be okay about getting some help—with trying to figure out what's going on. That's sure to come up when we get there. Mom is probably going to have some thoughts on what you ought to do or where you ought to go. I thought that if we had, like, a united front..."

"Sure I will," he said. "Look into things, I mean. I think that would be interesting. But I'm not going to any place like Gramercy Manor. I'm staying home, and Meesh and I'll look around and find out what's available—for both of us. I think what happened before was, I got worn out and everything got messed up—my thing with Lisa, the research I was trying to do, my course work, everything. I couldn't concentrate; I was a mess. So I let them talk me into the Manor. But it wasn't where I belonged. The place was full of know-it-alls—and nuts. I didn't need that kind of situation, and I don't now. I hope you can understand that."

"Of course I can," I said to him. Was I telling the truth? I think so, based on what I knew about—and my confidence in— him. "My main idea is that we've got to know exactly what we want to say to Mom. It seems to me that we ought to go light on all the details—about what you thought, about what the Sons thought, and a lot of the stuff that happened with them. She doesn't need to know all that."

The thing was: Mom was different from me; the less she knew, the better. I'd believed that before, and I believed it still.

Maybe it was a generation thing or something, but she was much more apt to push the panic button and put everything into the hands of the "experts." And face it—her whole relationship with Cam was different from mine. She was his *mother*, after all.

Cam nodded. "I very much agree," he said. "You're right. That's good. All she needs to know is that I'm seeing someone competent—'getting help,' as you just said. That should satisfy her. I want to know what's going on—what's real and what isn't. What I can expect, if anyone can tell me that. It's weird, but in some ways I was better off before, when I was sure about…like, everything. This not knowing is a bitch, Chris."

"I can really see that," I agreed. "But I *know* you'll get it worked out. I know that. There isn't *anything* you can't do." I could feel the tears come into my eyes and my voice get all chokey as I said that. I wasn't sad—at all—just full of feeling, and of love for him.

"You're the greatest, bro," he told me then. "You really are. You've done the most for me that anyone could do. I'm a really lucky guy."

At the same exact instant we both lunged forward and wrapped our arms around each other. This was a different kind of hug than the one we'd had on the hill going up to Art Honeycutt's. This one was total unencumbered joy.

chapter 30

Our united front was a real success. I'm not sure exactly why—although the "united" part must have helped. As did (I think) the fact that Cam seemed so much like the Cam my mother'd always known, and that I, in the end, had done what I set out to do. And chances are our both having suffered painful injuries in the course of our adventure probably made Mom be a little more laid back—though frequently solicitous.

Whatever the explanation, she accepted—perhaps with varying degrees of enthusiasm—the scenarios that Cam and I (and the girls) had agreed on. I think she was more than a little...wary of Michelle and Millie, but she clearly liked the idea of Cam being home and getting treatment here, rather than way off in the Berkshires. If she had other ideas of what he ought to do, she kept them to herself.

I was interested in how she related to me once our first round of excited and emotional greetings was over. I don't know quite how to put this, and I may be just imagining or not remembering right, but it seemed as if she treated me, in some respects, the way she used to treat my *father*. I'm not saying she deferred to me completely, but she didn't patronize me, either—act as if I were some kind of lesser being, not too bright.

She was, for instance, merely accepting when I gave her the word on my own medical situation. Once I'd gotten up the energy to face the facts, I couldn't pretend my shoulder was still getting better. The stupid thing was pretty well shot (no pun intended). So as Cam and Meesh set out in search of the kind of attention they needed, Millie and I paid a visit to the orthopedist recommended by our family physician. From him I learned I was an excellent candidate for a "partial replacement of my proximal humerus." What that meant in plain English was that the bullet had done a job on the end of that arm bone that goes into the shoulder socket. And so I needed, in effect, a new ball joint, made out of some man-made materials.

I didn't much like the sound of that. This was "major surgery," which would have to be followed by "extensive rehab"—and my shoulder might never feel as good as new.

But in a not-so-funny way, my knowing this was something that I simply had to do, and to endure—if I didn't want to keep on being as messed up as I was then—made it a lot easier for me to understand what Cam was going to go through. I was sure he didn't look forward to talking to shrinks and other mental-health people and having them prescribe a course of treatment that'd most likely include medications that would somehow "change" him. But with Meesh's help, he was going to try to do all that.

One day while the girls were back home packing—I doubt my mother *loved* the idea of their becoming our neighbors, but she didn't ever say that—Cam and I got to talking about our respective futures, short and long term. We both were normally

215

apprehensive, and we could tell each other that (though not Mom), but we both had hope as well.

Cam was nowhere near through with his education, he informed me. He thought he might study *drumming*, he said, all sorts of drumming, as done in different societies and eras—and its usefulness as an aid to meditation. And he said he had a bit of a yen to learn more about plant biology. "Wouldn't it be a kick," he said, "to help produce a supergrain, something that'd really have an effect on world hunger?" He also wondered if it was too late for him to take up chess and see if he could get to be the champion of somewhere. "Maybe if I moved to a place like Burkina Faso," he said, and laughed. "I doubt there'd be a lot of competition there."

"I don't have any idea what I want to do," I told him, "other than be happy. But I just read that everyone's ability to enjoy life—look at the good side of things—may have more to do with their *genes* than anything."

"Oh, I don't know," Cam said. "I have a belief that conscious *noticing* has the most to do with happiness. We need to see the little everyday realities, you know? And not just see them, *dwell* on them. Like, just for instance..." He leaned back in his chair and closed his eyes for a moment. "The unbelievable *liquidity* of water when your mouth is really dry..." He nodded, dwelling on that thought, I guess. "And a clean towel's smell, or some notes of music fitting into you just where you need them, or how being naked feels sometimes, and how loving someone changes everything...."

"And then there's the taste," I added, getting into it, "of a made-to-order, by yourself and for yourself, bacon, turkey, and tomato sandwich."

My brother smiled at that. We both did.

That exchange was like it used to be with me and Cam. He'd come up with something, and quite frequently, I'd find that it made sense to me.

"Maybe," I said then, carried away by nostalgia and trying to get a little fancy, "simple things like those are, after all, the golden needles in the haystacks of our lives."

I raised my eyebrows, seeking his agreement and approval.

"Pretty weak analogy," my older, wiser brother said.

Julian F. Thompson is the author of more than fifteen novels for young people, including the classic *The Grounding of Group 6* and *A Band of Angels*. The founder of an alternative high school and a teacher and coach for many years, Mr. Thompson lives in Vermont with his wife, Polly, a painter, and Reggie, a chocolate-colored mostly Lab.

THE WHITE MERCEDES

by Philip Pullman

A chance meeting with Jenny at an Oxford party leaves seventeen-year-old Chris with hope for a summer romance—and no premonition of trouble. Busy with his summer job and soon in love with Jenny, whose cheerful surface belies the dark uncertainty of her past, Chris misses all the signs of danger. Before he knows it, he's caught in the sinister web of a criminal whose desire for revenge crushes all those who stand in his way.

★ "Compelling…A modern-day Shakespearean tragedy."
—*Publishers Weekly* (starred review)

"An engrossing, tragic story with rare depth of feeling…Readers won't be able to turn the pages fast enough." —*Kirkus Reviews*

"Fans of Robert Cormier should appreciate this tense thriller." —*The Bulletin of the Center for Children's Books*

"The story line will hook readers and hold them….A page-turner that raises some unsettling questions about trust and betrayal and the nature of good and evil."
—*School Library Journal*